"What are you doing?"
Lucy demanded.

"Just trying to be accommodating." Caleb gave her a look of injured innocence. "I thought you objected to my being dressed while you were naked."

"What I object to is your being here in the first place."

"Now, that's not very kind of you," he said mournfully. "Especially since I was kind enough to bring you a brandy for shock."

"I haven't had a shock!" Lucy snapped. "Unless you're planning on providing one?"

"Tempting." He looked regretful. "I doubt I could find the energy to attack you—but, on the other hand, I'd be equally hard-pressed to put up much resistance if you were to throw yourself at me."

"You're safe," Lucy said dryly. "I never attack strange men on an empty stomach."

"Pity." He managed to look disappointed. "Tell you what, I'll feed you. Then we'll see what happens."

Dear Reader:

Two months ago we were delighted to announce the arrival of TO HAVE AND TO HOLD, the thrilling new romance series that takes you into the world of married love. We're pleased to report that letters of praise and enthusiasm are pouring in daily. TO HAVE AND TO HOLD is clearly off to a great start!

TO HAVE AND TO HOLD is the first and only series that portrays the joys and heartaches of marriage. Its unique concept makes it significantly different from the other lines now available to you, and it presents stories that meet the high standards set by SECOND CHANCE AT LOVE. TO HAVE AND TO HOLD offers all the compelling romance, exciting sensuality, and heartwarming entertainment you expect.

We think you'll love TO HAVE AND TO HOLD—and that you'll become the kind of loyal reader who is making SECOND CHANCE AT LOVE an ever-increasing success. Read about love affairs that last a lifetime. Look for three TO HAVE AND TO HOLD romances each and every month, as well as six SECOND CHANCE AT LOVE romances each month. We hope you'll read and enjoy them all. And please keep writing! Your thoughts about our books are very important to us.

Warm Wishes,

Ellen Edwards

Ellen Edwards
SECOND CHANCE AT LOVE
The Berkley Publishing Group
200 Madison Avenue
New York, N.Y. 10016

Second Chance at Love

TENDER TRAP
CHARLOTTE HINES

SECOND CHANCE AT LOVE
BOOK

TENDER TRAP

CHAPTER
One

"HE'S SEATED AT the table behind you and slightly to the left. The one beside the pillar. No, don't turn yet," the petite brunette cautioned, "one of the women is looking this way. Caleb Bannister is the striking-looking blond in the black evening jacket. It's okay, you can look now."

Obediently, Lucy Travers turned and casually regarded the group in question: six people, three of them exquisitely gowned women who appeared to have been cast from an identical mold labeled "glamour." She dismissed the women as unimportant; it was a man that Beth seemed anxious for her to see. Her gaze skimmed over a middle-aged man as well as a younger one in maroon velvet and pink satin frills and came to rest on the man who had to be Caleb Bannister.

He was conservatively dressed in conventional black evening wear. Its expert tailoring molded his powerful frame, outlining the truly impressive breadth of his shoulders. The pristine whiteness of his shirt highlighted a deep tan, which made a mockery of the popular fiction that blonds burn and peel. His rough-hewn features were dominated by a sharp blade of a nose and a square, uncompromising jaw. His ash-blond hair was cut slightly shorter than was fashionable—probably because of its tendency to curl, Lucy thought, noting the ruthlessly brushed-back waves. Since he was seated, it was impossible to determine his exact height, but she would have been willing to bet that he topped six feet by a good five inches.

1

Mentally Lucy corrected Beth's original description. Caleb Bannister looked much more than striking. He possessed that elusive something called presence. It wasn't simply his size or his undoubted wealth, she decided, although they both contributed to the overall effect. It was more the fact that he radiated authority. Caleb Bannister was undoubtedly a very powerful man. Not at all the type she herself would care to tangle with.

"Well?" Beth demanded impatiently.

"Well, what?"

"What do you think?"

"What's to think?" Lucy shrugged. "He looks like a reincarnation of one of those pictures of an early captain of industry. You know the type I mean. Lord of all he surveys. And he seems to have very expensive taste in women, if the blonde he's hanging over is his date. That's Maxine Fredon, isn't it? The star of that new comedy that opened on Broadway last week?"

"Yes," Beth confirmed, "and he can afford her. He's worth millions."

"So who's Caleb Bannister, and why are you so taken with him?"

"He's a venture capitalist..." Beth paused to give her words impact, "and he's my future husband."

"Your *what*?" Lucy gasped and quickly swiveled around to take a second look at the man. He was still giving his undivided attention to the actress. "Not very attentive to his future wife, is he?" Lucy asked dryly, turning back.

"Oh, he doesn't know it yet," Beth assured her in all seriousness. "We haven't met."

"God deliver me from another one of your harebrained schemes to capture a husband," Lucy said emphatically. "I still haven't recovered from last month when you convinced me to go with you to that great new singles bar you'd heard about, full of unattached males."

"Well, it was," Beth pointed out. "How was I to know that they were there for the gambling in the back room?

Or that the vice squad would pick that particular night to raid the place? I did offer to pay your fine."

"Or," Lucy continued, "from the fiasco the month before when you took me to a meeting of an organization full of eligible men without bothering to tell me that the membership was limited to degreed engineers. My God, I still get the shudders when I remember what it felt like when the moderator asked me to get up and give my opinion on the structural rigidity of something or other."

"You did look rather appalled"—Beth giggled— "and I will admit it must have been sort of embarrassing when everyone laughed."

"Sort of embarrassing! Try devastating!"

"But Lucy, it wasn't my fault. It was the tomatoes."

"Tomatoes?" Lucy questioned. Adroit though she had become at following her volatile friend's abrupt conversation changes, this time she was lost.

"You see, I read this article on how to catch a man, and the author used the analogy of tomatoes."

"Keep talking," Lucy instructed. "Sooner or later I'll see the connection."

"It's simple, really. If you know that the supermarket gets its weekly supply of tomatoes in on Friday morning, then to get the freshest ones, you should shop on Friday afternoon. If you wait until Thursday, all you'll get are the leftovers. The same thing holds true for men. If you want a selection of prime specimens, then you have to go to a place where they congregate. I figured that an engineering society would be full of men, and it was. Do you see?"

"Yes," Lucy nodded, "and that's what worries me. When your schemes start to make sense, I know I'm in trouble."

"But this time my idea's foolproof," Beth insisted. "I've thought this whole thing through. My problem is that I've been waiting for a likely-looking husband to appear, and that isn't a very efficient way of going about things."

"I don't know about efficient, but it certainly hasn't been very effective," Lucy said tartly.

"What I *should* do is pick out one man and concentrate on getting him to propose marriage."

"Supposing what you say is true, why pick someone like Caleb Bannister? Why not choose a man from the same background as yourself?"

"Because if I'm going to have to learn to love someone after I marry him, I might as well learn to love a rich man as a poor one," Beth said reasonably. "Besides, Caleb Bannister has been mentioned in the gossip columns lots of times over the past few years, and that's essential to our plan."

"Our plan?" Lucy arched a russet eyebrow.

"Lucy, you can't let me down now. Not after all we've been through."

"You mean because of all we've been through!" Lucy snapped.

"But you're essential to my plan," Beth pleaded. "I have to have your expertise on the computer."

"Computer?" Lucy frowned. "How does a computer fit into all this?"

"The computer is going to do the groundwork. I've collected all the information about Caleb Bannister that I could find. I went back five years and got every fact, both personal and business—and believe me, there was plenty. He has three files in the morgue."

"Morgue?" Lucy blinked.

"Newspaper morgue," Beth said impatiently. "Lucy, you aren't very alert tonight."

"It's my inbuilt sense of disaster working overtime. You still haven't told me exactly where I come into this."

"I want you to feed all the information I've collected into one of your computers. Then I want you to ask the computer questions. It should be possible to get a profile of Caleb's idea of the perfect woman. Once I know, I'll turn myself into his ideal, introduce myself to him, and, bingo, he should be caught before he knows what happened."

"Hmmm," Lucy murmured, her interest well and truly caught. She loved her job as a senior systems analyst at City Life in Manhattan. Computers fascinated her, and she was always interested in novel adaptations. Beth's idea was certainly novel.

"You could do it, couldn't you?" Beth asked anxiously.

"I don't see why not," Lucy said slowly. "It would really be a very simple program. Of course," she warned, "it would only be as accurate as your facts, and gossip columnists are notoriously liberal with their interpretation of the truth."

"I know," Beth agreed, "but some things are indisputable. Like the physical characteristics of the women he's dated, what they wore, what they do."

"True."

"Then you'll help?" Beth demanded.

Lucy looked into Beth's pleading blue eyes and knew she was going to agree even though her gut reaction was to avoid this ruse like the plague. But habits were hard to break, and she'd been trailing along in the wake of Beth's ludicrous schemes ever since Beth had arrived in New York City two years ago. She had appeared at Lucy's apartment door one September morning and introduced herself as the new occupant of the efficiency across the hall. Over coffee she'd explained that she didn't expect to be staying long, as she intended to find a husband. But it hadn't proved to be as easy as Beth had assumed. Simply because there were quite a few million people squeezed into the city, it didn't mean that husbands were to be had for the asking. Lucy had watched, partly in awe and partly in dismay, as Beth had tried to snare a man with every method known to woman—all to no avail. Lucy's own advice, based on the experience of a failed marriage, was that Beth ought to give serious consideration to the joys of single life. This wisdom had been flatly rejected, and Beth had thrown herself all the harder into her search.

Then, too, Lucy admitted to herself, she had not only liked Beth but also felt protective of her. Not that Beth really needed protection. That was simply an illusion fostered by her petite build and childlike singlemindedness. Still, despite the fact that Beth was only three years younger than Lucy's own twenty-seven, she seemed at times to be from another generation.

"What's he doing now?" Lucy asked curiously as she noticed Beth staring behind her.

"Dancing." Beth sighed.

Lucy casually turned and glanced toward the postage-stamp-sized dance floor. She'd been right about his height, she noted, as she picked out Caleb's tall form. Nestled against his broad chest was the tiny actress, her arms clasped behind his neck while his large hands spanned her narrow waist. They were barely moving on the crowded floor, seemingly content to merely sway in place.

"Dancing?" Lucy questioned acidly.

Beth blinked at Lucy's acerbic tone, and Lucy relented. "Sorry, it's just jealousy speaking. Men never dance with you like that when you're five-ten in your stocking feet."

"You are tall," Beth admitted, "but you're very well proportioned."

"*Junoesque* is the euphemism you're searching for," Lucy responded.

"You're not fat!"

"No, I'm simply well rounded in a society that worships a size eight—something I will never be. My bones are bigger than that. But tell me, am I right in assuming that the whole reason you chose this expensive restaurant was that you knew Caleb Bannister would be here?"

"Uh-huh." Beth nodded.

"How did you find out?"

"One of the junior secretaries in his office was in my

sorority at college. She's a gold mine of information about his personal habits—although she won't say anything about his business interests, of course."

"A fine distinction," Lucy said dryly.

"Quit changing the subject, Lucy. Will you help me?" Beth's pale blue eyes looked huge in her small, heart-shaped face as she gazed imploringly at her friend.

"Yes," Lucy said with a sigh, "I'll help. To be honest, the computer application sounds fascinating. I know they've used computers to predict how groups of people will react to a given situation, but as far as I know your idea is unique."

"Oh, *thank* you, Lucy." Beth grinned, her relief evident. "I just know this is going to work."

"Maybe." Lucy sounded doubtful. "Just remember that the computer is only as good as the information you put into it. Computers don't have original thoughts. They merely collate facts and then extrapolate, so make sure your information is accurate and as diversified as possible."

"I will," Beth promised. "I already have. When can you do it?"

"If you have all your facts ready by Saturday, I can do it in the morning."

"It's a deal," Beth hastened to agree.

Despite Lucy's optimistic expectations, she wasn't able to finish the program until the middle of the following week. She had run into several unforeseen difficulties that had taken her several days to iron out, working on both her office computer and home terminal, but finally the program had run successfully, and a clear-cut picture of Caleb Bannister's ideal woman had emerged. According to Lucy's computer, his dream was five foot one and a half, slender to the point of being skinny, a blonde with short, curly hair, in possession of perfect teeth, an unblemished complexion, emerald-green eyes, and was a fashionable dresser. She was a high school graduate with two and a half years of college from a large state university, and was in some way professionally connected with either the fashion industry or the live theater.

"Wonderful." Beth gloated as she read the printout Lucy handed her. "I'm absolutely perfect—or near enough not to matter."

"Uh-huh." Lucy tossed her briefcase on her beige sofa and poured herself a glass of chilled white wine. She took a sip, kicked off her shoes, and crossed the room; wiggling her toes into the sand-colored carpeting. "I swear that some August day I'm going to melt right into the asphalt and never be heard of again."

"Look at this, Lucy. I'm only half an inch taller than his ideal."

"I noticed his preference for small, slender women," Lucy observed without rancor. "Actually, you match up pretty well."

"Except that my eyes are blue and my hair is brown, but that's easily fixed."

"A wig?" Lucy peered at the offending hair over the rim of her wineglass.

"No," Beth shook her head, "too risky. It's liable to come off at a crucial moment. I'll make an appointment to have my hair bleached and permed. And I can get green contact lenses for my eyes."

"But you don't wear glasses!"

"It doesn't matter. You can get the contact equivalent of plain glasses. Actresses use them all the time. Now, let's see, it says his ideal has two and a half years at a state school."

"Ball State is a state school, isn't it?" Lucy sank down on the sofa.

"Yes, but I don't think that's what he means. Just to be on the safe side, I'll substitute two and a half years at Indiana University. It's a state school and, God knows, it's big enough."

"You'll have to change your profession too," Lucy pointed out, getting caught up in Beth's reasoning. "Dental hygienists don't turn him on."

Beth frowned. "Well, I can't say I'm an actress because he'd be bound to ask what I've worked in, and I can't say I'm a model because I've never been photographed."

"Why not say you're a dress designer working with one of the big houses?" Lucy suggested.

"I'll have to. I'll do some snooping around when I visit some of the dress salons tomorrow."

"Now that we've synthesized all this information, Beth, have you given any thought as to how you're actually going to make contact with the man?"

"Yes. You remember Maggie, the sorority sister who works in his office? She says he jogs every evening at about six-thirty in the park in front of his townhouse."

"You're planning on running into him?" Lucy couldn't resist the crack.

"We are," Beth corrected, rushing to explain at Lucy's horrified look. "You have to come with me, Lucy. It'll be too obvious if I go by myself. But he'll never suspect anything if there's two of us. After all, if you're planning on picking up a man, you don't take any competition along."

"I'm not competition," Lucy pointed out. "At least, not for Caleb Bannister. I'm eight and a half inches too tall, my curves are generous rather than slender, my hair is a carroty red and long, and furthermore, I've got brown eyes and freckles."

"But he doesn't know that we've got him figured out," Beth argued, "and you are a very attractive woman."

"But I don't jog, remember? That's your specialty."

"There's nothing to it," Beth dismissed her objections. "We'll simply do a short run around the park, let him get a glimpse of me, and then leave. I won't try to make contact until the second or third day."

"Should I live so long." Lucy moaned. "Tell me, just how big is this park?"

"Small. No more than a city block. Bannister has a

huge townhouse in the Murray Hill section of Manhattan, and this park is basically used by the residents. But it isn't closed or anything. I checked it out."

"How does Bannister feel about athletic women?" Lucy asked. "I never thought to ask the computer."

"Can you?"

"Sure." Lucy put down her drink. "Come on." She walked into her minuscule study and turned on her home terminal hookup.

"Lucy," said Beth, suddenly worried, "can anyone use our program? Someone at your office, I mean?"

"No. They'd have to know the password that activates the program."

"Password?"

"Marriage program." Lucy grinned. "There." She finished typing, pushed a button, and waited for the readout to light the green screen. "According to the computer, there are insufficient data to predict his response to a woman jogger."

"Ask it about women's sports in general."

"Okay." Lucy obediently keyed in the request. "His ideal woman rides for pleasure, using an English saddle, and there are insufficient data to extrapolate about other sports."

"Oh, great." Beth groaned. "I can't even ride when I've got that stickyup thing in front to hold onto."

"So stay away from horses," Lucy advised. "They aren't all that common in New York City."

Friday evening finally arrived, to Lucy's secret dismay. She didn't regret her involvement in the overall plan to help Beth capture Caleb Bannister, but certain parts of their plan were definitely giving her second thoughts. She slipped into her newly purchased jogging outfit and then grimaced as she studied her image in her bedroom mirror. Beth's assurances that her outfit was exactly what a serious jogger would wear had not made her feel any more comfortable.

The brevity of the black nylon shorts was bad enough, but the top was even worse. One eight-inch band of black nylon formed the top of the deeply cut tank top, while the bottom was silver netting. According to Beth, who'd bought a similar outfit in electric blue, the netting allowed the air to circulate—but Lucy had the unsettling feeling that it merely served to show off her body.

She picked up her hairbrush and began to brush her gleaming red hair, noting its shining condition with pleasure. Then she frowned at her image in the mirror as she tried to decide what to do with her tresses. Her usual chignon would never do; it would be hanging down around her ears before she'd gone once around the park. Briefly she considered leaving her hair loose, but discarded the idea. She couldn't stand hair flying in her face. About the only practical solution was a braid, she concluded; something she hadn't worn since the fifth grade. She quickly fashioned a single braid, securing the end with a rubber band, then flung the glowing rope over her shoulder and glanced at her cosmetics tray. What did the well-dressed jogger wear? She considered a variety of makeup before finally settling on just a touch of clear red lipstick.

The strident ringing of the doorbell alerted her to Beth's arrival, and Lucy hurried to open the door, eager to get this part of Beth's plan over.

Beth was standing in the hallway with tears streaming down her cheeks, her small face the picture of woe.

"Beth!" Lucy was appalled. "What's wrong? Why are you crying?"

"I'm not." Beth sniffed forlornly. "It's these contacts. I just got them this afternoon and they're driving me crazy! My eyes feel like someone poured sand in them, and they won't stop watering."

"Why don't you call the optometrist?" Lucy walked with Beth into the room.

"I did." Beth sank down onto Lucy's sofa. "He said the reaction will probably disappear in a few days and that I should try to keep them in for a short while each day so that my eyes can get used to them."

"I guess we won't be running tonight." Lucy tried not to show her relief.

"We can't postpone it!" Beth wailed.

"Beth, be reasonable. You're hardly going to appeal to Caleb Bannister with puffy red eyes—even if your new blond hairdo does look spectacular on you."

"It does look pretty good, doesn't it?" Beth patted her ash-blond mop of expertly cut curls, but she was only momentarily diverted. "We weren't going to try to make contact this evening anyway, Lucy. We were simply going to give him a tantalizing glimpse of me and check to make sure that Maggie's information about his running habits is correct."

"So?" Lucy asked, having a nasty suspicion where the conversation was heading.

"So why don't you do a few simple circuits around the park to look for him. Then, if Maggie was right about the time, we can go together next week. Please?"

"All right," Lucy capitulated, "by all means, let's check out Maggie's worth as a spy. But you're going to have to come with me. I'm not taking the subway over there dressed like this by myself."

Beth regarded Lucy's long, slim legs and said candidly, "You really look great. Kind of like"—she searched for inspiration—"like Diana."

"How appropriate." Lucy laughed. "Diana was the goddess of the hunt. Only I'm using a computer to capture our quarry instead of a bow and arrow."

"Much more practical," Beth agreed. "But we'd better hurry. It's getting close to six."

The Murray Hill townhouses facing the park were of aged red brick and were set flush with the sidewalk. Individual planters decorated some of the shallow steps, adding a distinctive touch of greenery. Altogether the area reflected a bygone era lovingly restored without a thought to anything so mundane as a budget or a mortgage. Beth's Caleb Bannister was indeed wealthy if he could afford to live in one of these architectural gems.

"Pretty, huh?" Beth commented as they walked from the subway station. "Although, to be honest, I'd much rather have something up on Seventy-second Street."

They reached the small park, set like an emerald in the midst of the drab city, and slipped inside. Beth took a seat on an unobtrusive park bench where she could wait for Lucy without being noticed.

"Go ahead," Beth encouraged Lucy. "Just remember to take it easy."

"Don't worry," Lucy answered wryly. She walked around the pathway for a few hundred feet, glancing covertly around for their quarry, but the only other people to be seen were an elderly man sitting on a bench reading the evening paper and a pudgy woman walking an equally pudgy Pekingese.

Drawing a deep breath, Lucy flipped her red braid behind her and began a slow jog. It was harder than she'd expected, and by the time she'd been once around the park her face felt fiery and her legs hurt. Gritting her teeth, trying to get her breathing under control, she began a second circuit. She was a quarter of the way around when she saw him. He must have come in by the other entrance to the park. She blinked and then, to get a better view, blew away some of the damp hairs that had escaped her braid and were sticking to her hot face.

He was worth a second look. And, she noted with relief, her jogging outfit was indeed normal. Bannister was wearing a skimpy pair of green nylon shorts that rode two inches below his waist and barely covered his lean hips. From the waistband up, the only thing he wore was sweat. His broad shoulders gleamed with it, and his iron-hard muscles rippled across his back as he ran. A thick pelt of dark blond hair covered his chest and narrowed down to disappear into his shorts. Bannister's muscular legs pounded out a steady rhythm as he approached and passed Lucy without so much as a nod.

So far the computer was right, Lucy acknowledged with a faint feeling of regret. Tall redheads didn't even impinge on his consciousness. Lucy had progressed another third of the way around the park when Bannister passed her again, his breathing depressingly regular.

Doggedly, Lucy kept running around the course as he passed her twice more. Finally, satisfied that Maggie's information had been correct, Lucy decided she would let him pass her one more time and then she would nonchalantly walk across the park to the opposite side where Beth was waiting. She kept moving until he was just beyond her and turned sharply. Unfortunately, while she had checked for other joggers, she hadn't thought to look down—and she entirely failed to see the fat Pekingese running along beside her. Her foot caught him in the ribs and, jerking sideways to get out of his way, she lost her balance and fell onto a park bench. She scraped her back on the bench's hard edge before tumbling onto the concrete pathway in a tangle of arms, legs, and furious teeth-snapping fur.

"Leave him alone!" a shrill voice screamed. "You clumsy jogger, trying to kill my poor little Ling Chow!"

"Lady," Lucy gasped, her accident not helping her breathless state, "I'm sorry. I didn't see him."

"Well, you should have. You could have killed him, great big thing like you landing on him!"

"I'm sure she didn't mean to frighten Ling Chow, madam," said a deep velvet voice behind Lucy.

"Hmphf!" The woman quite obviously had her doubts about it, but she allowed herself to be charmed and, with a sniff, gathered up the furiously yapping beast and walked off.

"Are you all right?" Hard hands plucked Lucy up as if she were Beth's size and effortlessly set her down on the bench.

"Yes, thank you." Lucy winced as the movement sent a thousand splinters of pain lancing through her body.

She glanced down and grimaced. She had landed heavily on her knees, and the concrete had lacerated them, leaving them bleeding. If possible, they felt even worse than they looked. Moreover, the left side of her back had been badly scraped on the end of the bench.

"Well, you sure as hell don't look it." Caleb Bannister's gentle fingers probed her knees and explored her back. "I wouldn't make any sudden movements if I were you." He chuckled. "You ripped your top on the bench, and it's held together by only a thread."

"Thank you," Lucy gritted out, feeling that having her top fall off would be a fitting finale to this debacle.

Caleb Bannister squatted on his haunches and took a closer look at her knees. He really was a magnificent specimen of a man. She could even wear heels, she mused, and not tower above him. *Stop it!* She pulled up her wayward thoughts as she realized where they were heading. Caleb Bannister was earmarked for Beth. Besides, he hadn't shown the slightest interest in her until she'd fallen—and even now he exhibited merely politely impersonal concern.

"You're relatively new to running, aren't you?" he asked.

"What makes you think that?" Lucy responded cautiously.

"Several things." Bannister smiled at her, his vivid blue eyes twinkling. "Your stride is atrocious, your shoes are brand-new, your breathing's erratic, and one of the first things a jogger learns is to watch out for dogs—especially little, bad-tempered ones."

"I didn't realize that my form was quite that bad." Lucy was piqued. She knew she hadn't looked like an expert, but surely she hadn't been as bad as all that.

"Oh, I wouldn't say your form's bad." Bannister rocked back on his heels and allowed his eyes to slowly caress her length. His bright blue gaze was like a physical touch, and Lucy felt her breathing constrict at the frank appreciation she saw in his eyes. "As a matter of fact, you're

in top form. At least, most of you is," he amended ruefully as the blood continued to drip off her knees. "Now
then, where do you live?" he asked briskly.

"Live?" Lucy repeated blankly, her mind still en-
meshed in the haze of sexual excitement he was pro-
jecting.

"You know—the place in which you reside between
suicide missions. Which house is yours?" He looked at
the row of townhouses ringing the park.

"Oh, yes." Lucy licked her dry lips and frantically
searched her mind for an answer. How would she explain
her presence here? There was no help for it. She'd have
to lie.

"I don't live around here. I noticed this park on my
way to work and decided it looked like a safe place to
run. So I had a friend drop me off," Lucy ad-libbed. "I
thought I'd run home afterward. You go right ahead,"
she dismissed him, intending to get back to Beth once
he was gone. "I'll just sit here and rest a minute."

"It's going to take longer than a minute before you're
in any shape to walk, let alone run. Besides," he added
when Lucy opened her mouth, "with your top coming
apart, you'd probably be arrested for indecent exposure
before you'd gone two blocks. Come on"—he sighed—
"someone obviously has to take care of you."

"I assure you, I'll be fine," Lucy snapped.

"Your track record isn't too good so far." Caleb Bannister got her to her feet by the simple expedient of
putting his hands under her arms and picking her up.

Lucy groaned as her scraped knees protested the
movement.

"And you intended to run home!" He snorted. "Come
on, woman, you can clean up at my place." He put an
arm around her shoulders and began guiding her out of
the park and across the street.

Lucy went, mainly because she wasn't sure what else
to do. She couldn't tell him the truth without giving the
whole game away, and she couldn't think of a believable

lie on such short notice. Besides, she consoled herself, they'd wanted to make contact with him—and they'd certainly done that. It merely remained to be seen whether they could turn this meeting to their advantage.

CHAPTER
Two

CALEB BANNISTER ESCORTED Lucy up the two broad red brick steps to the entrance to his town house and released her as he bent to remove his key from the zippered pocket in his running shoe. Lucy edged away, grateful to escape. She was by no means a prude, but being pressed against the hard, muscular length of him as he'd helped her along had done strange things to her equilibrium. She could still feel the warmth of her bare skin where he had touched her. Resolutely, Lucy tried to banish her physical reaction to him. She wasn't some callow adolescent to be thrown into a tizzy over the sight of a nearly naked man, no matter how well built he was.

Lucy studied his town house curiously. The gleaming black front door was set in a white door frame. Twin brass light fixtures were placed at eye level on each side of the entrance. The town house's soft red brick exterior was broken by two windows on each side of the door. It was huge, especially by Manhattan standards, with three full floors and a dormered attic above as well as a half-submerged basement. Lucy guessed that the lower level had originally held the kitchens, but from the closed walnut shutters it was impossible to tell what was housed there now.

The key turned with a well-oiled click and the massive door swung open to reveal an elegantly formal foyer.

"Come inside. Don't stand there dripping blood on my doorstep."

"I'm not!" Lucy snapped—but she obeyed, stepping

19

into the blissfully cool, air-conditioned room. "At least, not much," she amended honestly as she looked down at her lacerated knees.

"This way." He urged her up a magnificent cherry staircase. "We'll attend to your wounds upstairs."

Lucy went. Even though she had grave doubts about the wisdom of her actions, she didn't see what she could do about the circumstances without irreparably damaging their plan. She'd been so busy thinking of Caleb Bannister as an abstract entity—merely the focus of her programming and of Beth's ambitions—that she hadn't given much thought to Caleb Bannister the flesh-and-blood man. And a man he most definitely was, Lucy thought as she limped along behind his broad frame. But, she considered ruefully, she should be safe enough. Not only did his tastes run to petite blondes, but there had been nothing at all in the information she'd fed the computer to indicate that he was a libertine. He obviously enjoyed women's company and, presumably, their bodies, but he was neither flagrant in his seductions nor obsessed with the opposite sex.

Lucy got a vague impression of thick carpets and cool, restfully colored walls as he hustled her down a long hallway and through the last door on the right. She noted a huge, ornately carved bed, a broad expanse of sand-colored carpeting, and the vivid splashes of abstract paintings on cream-colored walls before he pushed her through a door. Lucy found herself in the biggest bathroom she'd ever seen.

"Sit down." He pointed to a brass stool. Lucy sat and watched as he flipped on the water taps in the bath, sending a flood of steaming water into the oversized, freestanding tub.

"Now, wait a minute." Lucy made an attempt to regain control. It wasn't like her to meekly follow orders, especially when those orders led her to a strange man's bathroom. But Caleb Bannister had that effect on her—and probably on most people, she thought shrewdly. His massive size, coupled with his winning and very forceful personality, would tend to swamp people's resistance. "I'm grateful that you've offered to help, but ..." She broke off helplessly and looked around the room.

Caleb Bannister followed her glance. "You don't like the decor. I'll admit that the mirrored walls and ceiling aren't everyone's cup of tea. Or the masks." He pointed behind Lucy and she automatically turned, letting out a gasp when her eyes lit on four hideous wooden masks mounted on the wall.

"That's most people's reaction"—he grinned—"but I'm rather attached to them. They're fertility symbols I picked up on a trip to Borneo."

"A psychiatrist would have a field day with that," Lucy said tartly, "and you know perfectly well it isn't the decor. Actually, it's rather appealing, but the point is that we don't even know each other."

"And here we are sniping at each other over the bathtub. But that's easily remedied. I'm Caleb Bannister, harmless bachelor."

Lucy snorted. Caleb Bannister was about as harmless as a Sherman tank.

"Lucy Travers," she introduced herself.

"Also a harmless bachelor?" He looked at her hopefully.

"The word is spinster—although I will admit that bachelor sounds better—and no, I'm not. I'm divorced."

"As for my bringing you home," he continued, "what would you do if you came across a dog that had been hit by a car? Wouldn't you take it home and try to patch it up?"

"I am *not* a dog!" Lucy objected.

"I'll say." His eyes roamed appreciatively down her figure. "But you are a fellow jogger. At least you'd like to be one. In fact, you don't do anything right, and from the way you were huffing and puffing I'd say you're out of shape."

"Thank you," Lucy said sourly.

"You never did tell me how long you've been running." He turned off the taps and flipped a switch to turn on the whirlpool unit.

Lucy watched the foaming bubbles with a fascinated eye. She'd never been in a whirlpool bath before. "Um, well, actually, tonight was my first time." She decided that the fewer lies she told, the easier it would be to remember what she'd said.

"The first time!" Bannister exclaimed. "Good God, woman, have you no brains! You're supposed to work up to things, especially in this heat."

"It seemed like a good idea at the time," she insisted, even though she knew he was right.

"So did Napoleon's march on Moscow, and look what happened to him."

"Napoleon?" Lucy gave him her best wide-eyed look. She didn't like being lectured at the best of times, but she could hardly tell him the facts behind her precipitous leap into the world of physical fitness. "Wasn't he the baker who invented those lovely gooey French pastries?"

"He did have a taste for French tarts," Caleb Bannister agreed blandly. He swirled his fingers in the foaming water. "Perfect," he pronounced and proceeded to wipe his wet hand across his broad chest.

Lucy's eyes followed his hand's movement, noting the water droplets which clung to his thick pelt of hair.

"You climb in and soak yourself. It'll do wonders for your knees, to say nothing of your muscles. You'll be sore as hell tomorrow. Take your time," he threw over his shoulder as he left.

Lucy breathed a deep sigh of relief. Alone at last. Now what? She looked at the swirling water and then down at her caked knees. It couldn't hurt to soak for a few minutes, just long enough to get the imbedded dirt out of the scrapes.

Lucy glanced at the door. It didn't have a lock, but she wasn't worried. Even if she hadn't already known that she wasn't Caleb Bannister's type, his manner would

have told her. Despite the compliments about her figure—which she had no doubt had been uttered in a kind
attempt to placate her feelings—he'd treated her more
like a hurt child than a desirable woman. Hadn't he, after
all, compared her to a dog?

Ah, well, Lucy consoled herself as she stripped off
her shorts and ripped top, simply because Caleb Bannister didn't find her attractive didn't mean that *all* men
went for small women. She might not be petite and delicate, but she did have something—just a shade too much
of it. Lucy eyed her figure in the mirrors. In a society
that preached that no woman could be too thin, her own
ample bosom and rounded hips were definitely out of
place.

Gingerly, she climbed into the foaming water, wincing slightly as the hot water washed over her knees. It
was heavenly to let the dancing waters swirl around her
body. Absolutely heavenly. The moving water was having a hypnotic effect, and she felt herself slipping into
a lethargic state of well-being.

Lucy leaned back against the tub and closed her eyes,
more than willing to let things drift for the moment. Her
contentment was rudely shattered when, without so much
as a perfunctory knock on the bathroom door, Caleb
Bannister entered.

"Close your eyes," he said cheerfully, adding unnec-
essarily, "I'm back." Caleb Bannister was much too over-
powering a physical specimen to ever pass unnoticed in
a crowd, let alone in a bathroom.

Lucy obediently closed her eyes and then immediately
opened them again. "What do you mean, close my eyes!
I'm the one who doesn't have any clothes on!" She slipped
further down under the water as she watched him walk
across the room. He was carrying a crystal brandy snifter
containing a goodly measure of an amber liquid.

"True." He grinned. "Your nudity doesn't bother me,
but if you'd prefer that we meet on equal grounds..."
He set the glass down on the rim of the tub and put his

hands on the waistband of his shorts.

"What are you doing?" Lucy demanded, although it was perfectly obvious what he was doing.

"Just trying to be accommodating." He gave her a look of injured innocence, as if he were an obliging host faced with an impossible guest. "I thought you objected to my being dressed while you were naked."

"What I object to is your being here in the first place."

"Now, that's not very kind of you," he said mournfully, "especially since I was kind enough to bring you a brandy for shock."

"I haven't had a shock!" Lucy snapped. "Unless you're planning on providing one?" She studied his muscular frame, which seemed even larger in the room's enclosed area.

"Tempting." He looked regretful. "But I'm afraid I'll have to turn you down."

"I wasn't asking, and you know it!"

"There's no reason to get upset," he said soothingly. "Normally, I'd be happy to oblige, but it's Friday."

"Friday?" Lucy was momentarily diverted, wondering if she and Beth had missed something in their programming. Nothing had come out of the computer about Fridays.

"Uh-huh—the Friday after a hell of a week." He nonchalantly rested one large shoe on the rim of the tub.

Lucy swallowed. Her breath caught in her throat as she studied the hard calf muscles at eye level. Almost of their own volition, her eyes followed the line of muscles to his lean, hard thighs and beyond. The thin, slightly damp nylon of his shorts did little to disguise his maleness. When Lucy realized where her errant thoughts were straying, she tore her gaze away.

"I doubt I could find the energy to attack you—but, on the other hand, I'd be equally hard-pressed to put up much resistance if you were to throw yourself at me." He looked at her expectantly.

"You're safe," Lucy said dryly. "I never attack strange

men on an empty stomach."

"Pity." He managed to look disappointed. "Tell you what, I'll feed you. Then we'll see what happens."

"That's not necessary," Lucy said, retreating. Things were going much too fast for her. All she'd set out to determine was whether he really did run in the evenings, and she'd wound up soaking in his whirlpool bath. "I wasn't hinting for a meal."

"Nonsense, I don't mind. I was going to send out for something anyway. What suits your tastes, pizza or Chinese?"

"Chinese," Lucy automatically answered.

"Good." He removed his foot and straightened up. "By the way, I left a shirt hanging on the door knob. Not that I'd mind your wearing your ripped top, but I thought you might be uncomfortable waiting for the final thread to separate."

"Thanks," Lucy answered with a grimace. "You're all heart."

"Not *all*." He smiled wolfishly at her, but to her relief didn't pursue the subject. "While we're eating, I'll outline a sensible running program for you."

"That's okay, you've done enough already."

"But I'd feel like I was turning a homeless waif loose if I didn't at least give you some advice. You obviously haven't the vaguest idea of how to set up training schedule. At your age you have to work up to things. It's dangerous to just leap into running."

"I'm only twenty-seven!" Lucy was outraged. He'd made her sound like she was middle-aged and fast approaching senility.

"That's old enough to know better. But don't worry, we'll have you in shape before you know it. By this time next year, you'll be training for the New York City marathon." And with that appalling idea, he left.

"Damn!" Lucy splashed the cheerfully bubbling water with the flat of her hand. Caleb Bannister had apparently taken it into his head to teach her running, and, short of a flat refusal on her part, he wasn't about to be deterred. An image of Beth's face formed in her mind. Beth would be counting on her. She couldn't flatly refuse. Lucy's accident had really been a stroke of luck for their plans, if not for her anatomy. But somehow Bannister's behavior seemed slightly out of sync with the computer readout. He'd been profiled as a very wealthy, conventional lawyer-turned-businessman. Dragging home wounded females didn't really mesh with that image—although Lucy supposed it did if you considered that he probably didn't see her as a woman at all, but merely as a fellow jogger, and a maladroit one at that.

The thought was curiously depressing, but Lucy forced herself to explore it. Everything pointed in that direction, even to the casual way he'd walked in on her in the bath without turning a hair.

Thoughtfully, Lucy picked up the glass and slowly sipped the brandy. She wrinkled her nose distastefully. Neat brandy wasn't her favorite drink, but right at this minute she felt the need of some Dutch courage.

It looked like she was stuck with the jogging, at least until she could manage to transfer his attention to Beth. For the life of her, Lucy couldn't understand what the attraction of running was. It was hot, sweaty, tiring, and, in her case, downright dangerous. She'd opt for a good brisk walk any day.

Lucy finished the brandy and climbed out of the tub, switching off the whirlpool unit. She shivered slightly in the cool air. The air conditioning had been marvelous after the hot, muggy humidity outside, but it was uncomfortable on wet skin. She used a caramel-colored bath towel to gently dab herself dry. She had a bad moment when the velvety terrycloth rubbed over her back and a sharp pain knifed through her. A glance in the mirrored wall showed a long, angry red welt running down her back.

Lucy slipped back into her brief shorts and then pulled

Caleb Bannister's thin cotton knit shirt over her tousled head. The shirt looked ridiculous on her. Designed for a broad man of six-five, it engulfed her, the shoulders coming halfway to her elbows and the hem completely covering her shorts. But she rather enjoyed the unaccustomed feeling of being relatively small. Even her ex-husband had been only half an inch taller than she.

Briefly, Lucy considered brushing out her mussed braid, but decided against it. Bannister might think she'd been primping, and she wanted to keep things very casual, with no hint of any man-woman feelings between them. That way she could hand him over to Beth without a pang. The thought disturbed her, and she chastised herself. But she did have a problem. Now that she'd met him, she liked him. The object of Beth's fantasies had turned out to be an extremely engaging man with feelings and desires of his own, and Lucy found herself strangely drawn to him. It was an attraction that she would have to ignore—for not only had Beth seen him first, but also, given his preferences, there was no way he would ever notice her as a desirable woman.

Thinking of Beth suddenly made Lucy wonder what had happened to her. From across the park Beth would have seen Lucy's clumsy stumble over the Pekingese, as well as her subsequent rescue. The question was, what had Beth done? Was she still waiting at the park for Lucy's return, or had she gone home to await further developments?

Lucy made her way back through the luxurious bedroom, not pausing to look around, although she would dearly have loved to. She was afraid that Caleb Bannister might return and catch her at it. She had no desire to be thought snoopy. Quickly she traversed the hallway and hurried down the stairs.

Bannister was in the foyer when she reached the bottom.

"There you are," he greeted her. "I was beginning to

think you'd drowned yourself." He frowned slightly as he looked at her knees. "Come along and I'll spray some antiseptic on your cuts."

"Do you mind if I make a call first?" she asked, noticing a phone on the entryway table. "The friend who dropped me off will be wondering what happened to me if I don't show up soon," she improvised.

"Go ahead," he answered genially. "I'll take you home when we've eaten. I need to pick something up at the office later anyway. I'll be in the sitting room in the back. Join me when you've finished."

"Thank you." Lucy gave him a weak smile. She dialed slowly, watching as he walked down the hallway and disappeared into a room on her left. The phone rang once before it was answered by a frantic-sounding Beth.

"Hello, Beth." Lucy carefully made her voice sound casual. She didn't think Caleb Bannister could hear her, but she didn't want to take any chances. Everything she'd read about the man had portrayed him as a very astute, intuitive person, and Lucy didn't want to make him curious about her actions. If he became suspicious, their plan might be jeopardized.

"Lucy!" Beth shrieked. "Where are you? I didn't know what to do, so I took a cab home to wait for you to call."

"Don't worry if I'm slightly late getting back," Lucy replied. "I had a slight accident, and a fellow jogger kindly took me home so that I could patch myself up."

"That was Caleb Bannister, wasn't it?" Beth demanded.

"That's the one," Lucy agreed. "He's going to bring me home later, so you have nothing to worry about."

"I'm not so sure about that," Beth said darkly. "Are you there alone with him?"

"Yes, but don't worry." Lucy laughed. "He assures me that he never attacks women on Fridays."

"What!"

The doorbell chimes interrupted, and Lucy hurriedly cut short her conversation as Caleb Bannister appeared.

"'Bye, Beth. I'll give you a call later."

"The *second* you get in!" Beth ordered.

Lucy gently returned the receiver to its cradle and stood by as Bannister opened the door to admit a teenaged boy delivering their dinner. The boy's eyes slid over Lucy's tall frame, garbed in Bannister's oversized shirt, and he gave her a knowing leer that made her long to smack him.

"It's all there, Mr. Bannister." The boy pocketed his tip.

Bannister nodded, closing the door behind him.

"Come on, Lucy." He transferred the large white sack to his right hand and reached for her arm. She pretended not to see the gesture and started down the hall. She wasn't sure why, but she didn't want him to touch her.

The sitting room turned out to be a large room at the very back of the house. Two sets of French doors, which opened out onto a brick-lined patio and glorious flower beds, flooded the room with light even at this time of the evening. Warm, cream-colored walls and a huge cream-and-yellow Aubusson carpet set a light, cheerful tone. What looked like a fully functioning ivory marble fireplace highlighted one wall, and placed in front of it, facing each other, were two sofas printed in yellow, cream, and spring green. Lucy headed for one of the sofas and sank down into its feathery softness.

Caleb set the bag down on the cherry coffee table between the sofas and reached for an aerosol can already sitting there.

"Let me see those knees." He leaned over and peered down at the offending parts. "It's not as bad as I originally thought, but I'll still spray some antiseptic on it just to be on the safe side. By next week you'll be as good as new."

She had doubts about that. As sore as her legs felt, she wasn't sure she'd ever walk again, let alone run. "Augh," she gasped as the icy spray of the antiseptic hit her knees. "That hurts!"

"Don't be such a coward," Caleb admonished her. "Keep a stiff upper lip."

"I'm under no obligation to keep a stiff upper any-thing," Lucy snapped, retreating along the sofa as he started shaking the can again.

"What are you *doing*?" She pushed his hand away as he tried to pull up her shirt.

"I'm trying to put some medicine on your scraped back," he told her, "and I wish you'd quit being coy. Dinner's getting cold. I assure you I have no designs on your body."

"I know; it's Friday," Lucy said, a little glumly, "and I'm not being coy."

"Then turn around and let's get this over with. I'm hungry."

Definitely not the words of a man bent of seduction, she acknowledged with faint regret as she turned around.

Caleb pulled the shirt up to her shoulders and ran gentle fingers down the sides of the long scrape. Lucy felt tiny shivers of awareness spark into life at the contact, shivers that grew and spread, constricting her breathing and twisting her stomach. She focused on a large yellow flower on the back of the sofa and tried to banish the sensation of his touch on her unexpectedly responsive body. The man was a master at the art of sensual arousal even when his interest was purely impersonal.

Lucy felt the icy, stinging spray with gratitude. She wanted no more intimate contact with Caleb Bannister than was absolutely necessary.

"There." He released her shirt and set down the can. "At least you won't get an infection."

"Thank you," Lucy replied formally, feeling unsure of her reactions to this man. He was in fact a stranger, but because of the program she'd written about him she felt as if she knew him quite well—to say nothing of the fact that she'd sat in his bathtub and passed the time of day with him while totally naked.

"You're welcome." He smiled at her, and she blinked

as the full force of his charm hit her. The man used his masculinity like a weapon, and she was willing to bet that in this case, at least, it was unintentional.

He broke into her thoughts. "Unpack dinner while I get some plates."

Lucy obligingly emptied the sack, setting the six white cartons on the table. Did he really expect them to eat all this? There was enough for a dinner party.

"What's the matter?" Caleb asked, returning. "You're looking at the food as if you've discovered bugs. I thought you said you liked Chinese cooking."

"I do, but so much? I assure you that just because I'm five-ten doesn't mean that I eat like a horse."

Caleb shot her a curiously penetrating glance and handed her a beautiful Haviland china plate and what seemed to be sterling-silver utensils.

"There's absolutely nothing wrong with a healthy appetite." Caleb began spooning rice onto his plate. "Especially when you've been exercising. I hope you aren't going to be one of those women who nibble on salads, moan about calories, and make me feel guilty when I eat a hearty meal."

"Well, maybe I can oblige," Lucy said lightly, following his lead and helping herself from the cartons.

"You've got a gorgeous figure, Lucy"—Bannister managed to inject a great deal of sincerity in his voice— "and I should know. Between that jogging outfit and the bath, I've seen most of it. As a matter of fact, if it weren't Friday, I'd be tempted to show you exactly what I think of it."

"You're too kind," Lucy said demurely, feeling cheered by his nonsense even though she was perfectly aware that he was only being polite. One thing the computer hadn't registered was that Caleb Bannister was a very nice man.

"And you, my dear Lucy, have an inferiority complex a mile wide. What's the matter, didn't your ex-husband like big women?"

"Marcus?" Lucy looked startled. "As a matter of fact, I doubt that he ever noticed what kind of shape I had. And I do not have an inferiority complex. I might be slightly defensive," she admitted at his disbelieving look, "but you would be, too, if you lived in this culture."

"I thought I did."

"I meant if you were your size and a woman. Take a look around you sometime. Desirable women are always depicted as small and in need of protecting. It's hard for a man to think of someone as being cuddly and sexy when she's as tall as he is."

"But you aren't."

"Aren't what?"

"Aren't as tall as I am," he repeated patiently. "I'm a good seven inches taller than you are, to say nothing of being quite a bit heavier."

"It may have escaped your notice, but there aren't too many men like you around," Lucy said tartly.

"I know." He smirked. "I'm unique."

"That's not necessarily a compliment," Lucy shot back and then took a large bite of her dinner. She was about to swallow when all of a sudden her mouth felt as if it were on fire. Desperately, she gulped the food down, but that only made things worse, spreading the burning down her throat and making her eyes water. She took a frantic look around, and Caleb, realizing her plight, handed her a crystal goblet full of red wine.

Lucy gulped the wine with complete disregard for its delicate bouquet. All she was concerned about was quenching the terrible burning.

"What was *that?*" she demanded hoarsely when the glass was empty and she could talk again.

"A Bordeaux," he began innocently, but Lucy cut him off.

"That's not what I meant and you know it. I've never even had Mexican food that hot."

"You don't need chili powder to get spicy food," he said smugly. "I thought you said you liked Chinese food."

"I do, but I usually eat either Double Happiness or moo shu pork and, believe me, they don't taste anything like that!"

"Beef in black bean sauce," Caleb enlightened her. "I suppose I should have warned you that some Chinese dishes tend to be a little hot."

"A little hot! Let me guess. You're one of those people who describe a war as a confrontation?"

"Try the beef and broccoli." Bannister pushed a carton toward her. "It's very bland."

"Thank you." Lucy peered suspiciously into the carton. It looked harmless enough, but then so had the other.

"Here." He took her plate and scraped the remaining beef in black bean sauce onto his dish, then he handed it back to her.

It seemed curiously intimate to be sharing food from each other's plates, but Lucy didn't want to explore the thought as she helped herself to the beef and broccoli.

"Tell me what you do," Caleb said as he refilled her wineglass.

"I work with computers." Lucy cautiously bit into her meal, realizing with relief that it was delicious.

"Doing what?"

"As a senior systems analyst." Lucy watched in awe as he ate the beef in black bean sauce without so much as a shudder.

"It's an acquired taste." He grinned, having no trouble reading her thoughts. "How did you get into computers?"

"By accident. My major in college was art history. I took a computer course to learn about the filing and classification of pictures and found I liked the computer better than the history. So after I graduated, I found a job as a programmer."

"Do you have any children?"

"No," Lucy replied shortly. That had been one point on which her usually vague husband had been firm. He'd absolutely refused to even consider children and, seeing the way their marriage had ended, he'd been right. But

Lucy still wished she'd had one. She loved children.

As if sensing her unwillingness to discuss that topic further, Caleb changed the subject, giving her a hilarious account of a would-be chemist who had wanted money for research into a perpetual youth serum.

"What exactly do you do?" Lucy asked curiously. The information Beth had given her had listed his profession as venture capitalist, but no details had been included. Almost all of Beth's facts had dealt with either his various girlfriends or his social preferences.

"I'm a venture capitalist. I got into the field when I was a corporate lawyer. I saw lots of men with really good, viable ideas who couldn't get them off the ground because they didn't have the vaguest idea where to go for financing. That's where I come in. I match available sources of money with the people who need it. You might say my specialty is being able to separate the wheat from the chaff."

"Oh?" Lucy nervously sipped her wine. There was a speculative gleam in his eyes that worried her. He was a highly intelligent man. But no man, no matter how smart, was a match for a full-sized computer, she comforted herself—especially when he didn't even realize that he was being manipulated by a computer.

CHAPTER
Three

LUCY HAD NO more than slipped out of Caleb's shirt and her running shorts when her doorbell rang.

"Blast!" she muttered as she hurriedly threw on a jade-green satin robe. Could that be Caleb Bannister—and if so, why? He'd dropped her off at the entrance of her apartment building not ten minutes ago, and he had shown no desire to come up with her. Not surprisingly, of course. Not only was she not his type, but she had also caused him no end of trouble.

"Just a minute!" she shouted as the strident bell chimed again. She tied the belt and ran to open the door, being careful to keep the safety chain on. Nine years of living in New York had made her very cautious.

Beth's small features, alight with curiosity, faced her through the opening.

"Just a second, Beth." Lucy shut the door, released the chain, and then opened it again to let her friend in.

"Well, what happened?" Beth erupted into the room. "What'd he do? What'd he say? Gosh, Lucy, I've been waiting all evening for you to get back! I have to hand it to you. Falling down was a great idea for getting his attention."

"I hate to disillusion you," Lucy said dryly, "but it was entirely unintentional. I might be committed to helping you catch a husband, but there is no way I'm going to sacrifice my body in the process."

"Oh, you poor thing," said Beth, genuinely sympathetic. "No wonder your tumble looked so real. Did you hurt yourself?"

"A couple of bruised knees." Lucy deliberately minimized her aches and pains. "I was about to make myself a cup of coffee. Would you like some?"

"Lucy!" Beth wailed. "Forget the coffee and tell me what happened after he helped you up. I was afraid to follow you for fear he might see me."

"Nothing," Lucy replied as she filled the kettle with hot water and put it on the burner.

"Nothing what?"

"Nothing happened," Lucy elaborated, conveniently forgetting the scene in the bathroom. "At least, nothing relevant."

"But you were gone for hours. What'd you do?"

"Well, he lent me a shirt, fed me some supper, gave me a lecture on the pitfalls of running, and then brought me home." Lucy felt strangely reluctant to discuss Caleb Bannister with Beth, but she forced herself to ignore the feeling. After all, he was Beth's idea and Beth's prospective husband, if Lucy's own program bore fruit.

"Honestly, Lucy," Beth said with a sigh, "getting information out of you is like pulling teeth! What was the house like?"

"Gorgeous," she replied truthfully, "absolutely gorgeous. It's a huge, four-story townhouse bordering the north end of the park. It's the kind of place with ankle-deep carpeting, priceless antiques, and real paintings."

"And loaded with old family retainers, I'll bet," Beth guessed. "Was there a reproduction of Jeeves the Butler?"

"Now that you mention it, there wasn't a single servant around." Lucy frowned thoughtfully. "Except for me and him, there was no one else there—but they have to be somewhere, because a house that size doesn't keep itself clean."

"I wonder what he does for food." Beth was diverted.

"Sends out. At least, that's what he did tonight."

"But what about Bannister himself?" Beth returned to the original subject. "You were with him for *hours*. You must have formed some opinion."

"Yes"—Lucy nodded—"I thought he was very nice."

"Nice!" Beth gasped. "You spend the evening closeted with one of the most powerful men on the New York financial scene, and you think he's 'very nice'?"

"Well, he is." Lucy sedately poured the boiling water over the instant coffee. "Kind, too. He didn't have to help me up or take me home. He could have just ignored me when I fell over that wretched little dog."

"Maybe he fancied you." The thought had obviously just occurred to Beth, and she sounded uncertain.

"Nope," Lucy replied cheerfully. "He never so much as made a pass." And God knows he had the opportunity, Lucy thought unhappily. "Besides, you know what the computer said. He likes small blondes with green eyes. Do I look like a small anything?"

"No." Beth sighed. "I guess I was simply jealous of you there for a minute."

"Don't be. He didn't even regard me as a woman, let alone a desirable one. To him I was just a fellow jogger who'd met with an accident. Believe me, he was much more interested in my mangled knees than in my feminine attributes."

"But it's still great that it happened," Beth insisted. "My contacts are feeling better by the minute, so tomorrow when you go jogging, I'll go, too, and you can introduce me."

"No." Lucy flatly rejected the idea. "There is no way that I'm going out jogging again until my knees heal— and not even then, if I can help it. For the life of me, I can't understand your enthusiasm for the sport. On top of all the obvious disadvantages, it's dangerous."

"You get adept at dodging cars and dogs."

"I'm pretty adept at avoiding muggers, but that doesn't mean that I make a practice of walking in Central Park after dark," Lucy said tartly.

"But Lucy, you said you'd help."

"And I will." Lucy hobbled into the living room and sat down. "But before we meet Caleb Bannister again I want to program everything I learned about him into the computer."

"Such as?" Beth asked curiously.

"Mostly odds and ends of information, like his passion for hot Chinese food, his whirlpool bath, the lack of visible servants. That kind of thing."

"None of that sounds very important to me." Beth sounded dubious.

"Taken by itself, it isn't," Lucy agreed. "But added to what we've already got programmed, it might be. Then again, it might not. All I know for certain is that the more facts we can give the computer, the better chance it has of doing what we want."

"So what do we do now?" Beth asked.

Lucy sipped her steaming coffee and stared into space for a moment. "Dinner, I think."

"You mean get him to ask us out for dinner?"

"No, I mean ask him here. We could have a dinner party, say . . . next Friday. I could say the invitation is a thank-you for having rescued and fed me. It's a normal enough gesture and, if we wait a week, it won't look like I'm chasing him."

"Which we are." Beth giggled.

"Which we are," Lucy concurred.

"Do we invite another man, or just have the three of us?" Beth asked.

"I think eight would be a better number," Lucy said.

"But why?"

"Because if you and I are the only women present, he's going to draw one of two conclusions. Either I'm chasing him or I'm pushing him at you—and you know the program was very specific about the fact that he likes to do his own pursuing. Any sign that he's the quarry and he'll disappear."

"But *eight?*"

"Eight is a good number," Lucy defended her choice. "It's big enough to avoid all appearances of an intimate little gathering and yet small enough to fit comfortably into my living room."

"I guess." Beth looked around the comfortable living room with its attached dining room. "We'd best use your apartment. My little efficiency is crowded with just me in it. So who do we invite?"

"No petite blondes," Lucy quipped.

"Be serious," Beth begged.

"I'm trying, but except for the computer application, which I take very seriously, this whole venture seems more like a cross between a Noel Coward play and a Three Stooges movie."

"I don't see why," Beth countered, defending her idea. "People meet and marry for all sorts of weird reasons. All we're doing is applying a scientific method to what is basically a game of chance. It's no wonder the divorce rate is so high, when you consider how haphazard the usual methods of finding a spouse are. You have to depend on fate, relatives, or the singles scene. Fate is notoriously fickle, the singles bars are basically clearinghouses for finding a quick bed partner, and when I think of some of the gems my relatives have come up with . . ." Beth shuddered.

"Amen!" Lucy said with heartfelt agreement, remembering her family's part in her own failed marriage.

Beth looked curiously at Lucy but refrained from asking more questions.

"So who do we invite?" Beth asked again.

"You, me, and Caleb Bannister, of course, and then I think one married couple. How about Jane and Tom Glasson?"

"Tom's in banking, so he can talk to Caleb about finances," Beth agreed.

"Tom's a vice president in charge of corporate loans," Lucy elaborated. "That's why I thought of him. We don't want Bannister bored."

"I'll take care of keeping him amused," Beth said confidently.

"No doubt," Lucy concurred, but strangely the thought brought no pleasure to her. "Then," Lucy forced herself to continue, "we'll have Linda Adams and John Vandasen. They aren't married, but they're living together, so Linda shouldn't give you any competition."

"And she's a brunette," Beth said with satisfaction.

"And, finally, I think Bob Herring, to round out the numbers. He's charming, bright, articulate, and he hates blondes so he shouldn't try to cut Bannister out with you."

"Hates blondes?" Beth was momentarily diverted. "Why?"

"His ex-wife was a blonde and she really took him to the cleaners when they were divorced," Lucy replied absently. "Is Friday night all right with you?"

"Fine. That will give me that much more time to get used to my contacts."

"Beth, what are you going to do if you ever do get him to marry you? Go through life wearing contacts you don't need?"

"When I get him to marry me," Beth corrected her. "And the answer is no. Once the knot is safely tied, I'll simply give them up. Since he doesn't know that I was wearing them only to trap him, he can hardly say anything when I quit."

"I guess." Lucy set her empty mug down on the end table and yawned. All the unaccustomed exercise on top of a hard day's work had exhausted her.

Beth must have noticed the unusual pallor of her skin. "Oh, dear, you look all done in, Lucy. Why don't you go to bed? We can finish our plans in the morning."

"An excellent idea." Lucy smiled sleepily.

By Friday morning, Lucy had everything under control. Her apartment gleamed, and from the office she made arrangements to pick up the centerpiece at the florist's on her way home from work. For a moment she remembered the marvelous flowers in Caleb's walled yard, and she sighed with envy. It would be wonderful to be able to simply go outside and pick flowers whenever you wanted. Although Lucy loved New York City and wouldn't live anywhere else, she wasn't blind to its faults, lack of space being one of them. Caleb Bannister had the best of both worlds: a huge home and a good-sized yard in a space-starved city.

Lucy had thought a great deal about the menu, trying to balance the calorie-counters' wants with her own love of cooking. She'd finally settled on a fresh shrimp cocktail, a simple beef rib roast, asparagus spears with an optional hollandaise sauce, baked potatoes, and for dessert a choice of either a fresh fruit compote or a sinfully rich Sacher torte. The meal had the added advantage of not requiring a lot of last-minute preparations.

Despite her careful planning, by the time evening came Lucy was running late. She'd hoped to be able to leave work early but instead, thanks to a foul-up in the payroll system, had wound up missing lunch and having to stay an hour over. She only hoped she'd managed to patch the system well enough for it to hold until Monday, when she could find out what the problem really was.

Lucy set her magnificent centerpiece of freesias down on the beige carpeting in the hall while she rummaged through her purse for her key. It took three tries before she was able to locate the elusive thing, and she was ready to scream with vexation. She was hot and tired and her head ached. The last thing she wanted to do after a busy Friday was entertain, but there really had been no choice about which evening to hold the dinner party. So many people left the city during the weekends to escape the stifling heat of August that she would have been hard-pressed to come up with enough dinner guests on a Saturday night.

Lucy finally got the key into the lock and turned it, pushing the door open before bending to pick up her flowers. The air in the apartment seemed hot and stuffy, and she frowned. She must have turned the air-conditioner down too far before leaving for work. She placed the flowers in the middle of her perfectly set dining room table before checking the thermostat in the living room. It was set for seventy-six, but it seemed much warmer than that to Lucy so she pushed it down to sixty-eight, for once ignoring energy conservation. The air conditioning obediently leaped into life, pouring chilly air out of its ducts.

Lucy sighed thankfully as the cold blast rolled over her hot feet.

She popped the roast in the microwave, turned it on, then opened a bottle of soda and gulped it down. She didn't think she'd ever get used to the humidity of August.

"Lucy?" Beth's voice came from the open doorway.

"Come on in and close the door behind you," Lucy called. "I just got in."

Beth was carrying a peck basket filled with tomatoes and another basket filled with raspberries, and was pushing a third full of green beans and carrots.

"Yum." Lucy took the basket of berries and immediately filched a handful. "Thanks, Beth! Where did you find all this? I'll have to add a few of these to the fruit compote."

"Lucy," Beth burst into speech, "Bob Herring called. He said his wife unexpectedly agreed to let him have his kids for the weekend. He said he was sorry to cancel at the last minute, but he knew you'd understand."

"Damn!" Lucy muttered. "I certainly don't begrudge him the time with his kids, but why couldn't his wife have gotten generous last weekend? Now we'll be a man short."

"No, we won't," Beth assured her. "I already asked someone else."

"Who's that?" Lucy asked idly as she put the vegetables in the refrigerator.

"It's stuffy in here." Beth seemed to notice the heat for the first time.

"I usually turn the thermostat up when I go to work. I guess I flipped it further than I thought this morning. Don't worry, it'll be cool by the time everyone arrives. Now, who did you invite to take Bob's place?"

"The gorgeous hunk who brought all this stuff for you."

"What gorgeous hunk?" Lucy stopped rearranging the refrigerator and turned to stare at Beth. If she hadn't provided the bounty, then...

"Good Heavens, Lucy...he isn't a stranger. You know who I mean. He's about your height, well built, black hair, blue eyes, handsome. I've seen him here lots of times, and besides, he said this stuff was from your mother. His name is Matt...Mark..."

"Marcus," Lucy supplied weakly. "Marcus Blackmore. Let me guess. He accepted. It's been that kind of a day."

"Yes, he did," Beth said uncertainly. "He seemed quite glad to. He said he'd been on vacation the last two weeks and didn't have a thing to eat in the house. What's wrong? Does he eat peas with his knife? Drink too much? Flirt with the men instead of the women?"

"No." Lucy groaned. "When he remembers, his manners are excellent and he's perfectly normal. Unfortunately, he also happens to be my ex-husband."

"What?" Beth shrieked. "You were married to him? But he visits you all the time."

"Why not?" Lucy asked irritably. "It was a perfectly civilized divorce. As a matter of fact, sometimes I think he forgets we ever got it. Hell!" Lucy slammed the refrigerator door. "That's exactly what this dinner party needed to liven it up: my ex-husband."

"I'm sorry, Lucy," Beth apologized. "I never would have invited him if I'd known. It must be very painful for you."

"You've been watching too many afternoon soap operas, Beth. I am not harboring any unrequited love for him, or he for me. As a matter of fact, I doubt if we ever did love each other."

Lucy picked up her half-empty soda and walked into the living room, plopping down on the sofa.

"Then why'd you get married?" Beth asked reasonably.

"Stupidity on my part and indolence on his." Lucy frowned, remembering. "I don't think he actually cared one way or the other about being married to me as long as he was left alone. You see, Marcus and I grew up in a small town upstate called Litton. We lived next door to each other. His folks were my godparents and mine were his. All our lives we heard, 'Isn't it cute how Marcus and Lucy love each other?' After about fifteen years, I began to believe it."

"What about Marcus?" Beth asked.

"Marcus has exactly one love in his life: microbiology. He literally lives and breathes the stuff. Anything else barely impinges on his consciousness. Of course, I was too young and self-centered to see that the only reason he escorted me places was because I was handy and our parents were pushing it. When I graduated from high school, our parents began urging us to marry. Marcus was a senior at Columbia, and they started talking about how we could find an apartment and live off campus. It all sounded so romantic." Lucy snorted. "Idiotic, more likely. Anyway, I was all for it, and Marcus didn't really care."

"So you got married?"

"So we got married," Lucy confirmed, "and by the time the honeymoon was over I knew we'd made a horrible mistake. We had absolutely no point of contact except our families. So I threw myself into working on my degree, and Marcus started his doctorate." Lucy paused.

"So what finally happened?"

"It was the white mice," Lucy said obscurely.

"White mice!"

"Once Marcus got his Ph.D., we moved out of the apartment and into a split-level on Long Island. He got a job at the medical center and started doing experiments at home in our basement. He had hundreds of white mice down there."

"Yech." Beth grimaced.

"They aren't so bad, as long as you've got good ventilation. Anyway, after about a year and a half, I started to have nasty asthma attacks. I couldn't breathe, and my eyes would swell shut."

Beth hazarded a guess. "The mice?"

"Yup. I went in for tests. I'll never forget the look on Marcus's face when the allergist told him either the mice went or I went."

"He chose the mice!" Beth was horrified.

"I didn't give him the chance." Lucy laughed. "I'd known for years that we were completely mismatched, but I'd lacked the courage to do anything about it. I decided that there was no reason for Marcus to give up his home research simply for the sake of a dead relationship. So I moved out and filed for divorce."

"Didn't he try to talk you out of it?"

"No. He was as aware of our mistake as I was. He just hadn't cared enough to do anything about it."

"But he seems to like you," Beth protested.

"He does," Lucy explained patiently, "and I like him. But I don't love him; neither do I understand him. He's not the world's easiest dinner guest. He has a bad habit of giving his partner chapter and verse of his latest research—and some of his research is hardly dinner-table conversation."

"Oh, dear, what do we do now?" Beth glanced at the clock. "They'll be here in fifty minutes."

"There's nothing we can do." Lucy shrugged. "I'll seat Marcus at my end of the table and hope for the best. Right now we'd both better get ready. What are you wearing?"

"Black. It's supposed to be his favorite dress color."

"Hmm." Lucy nodded. "A blonde in black."

"Wait until you see it, Lucy. It sure is sexy. It has a tiny lace bodice with ultrathin straps and a very full chiffon skirt. I bought a pair of fantastically expensive black leather sandals to wear with it. They're nothing more than a couple straps of thin leather and four-inch heels."

"Sounds promising," Lucy approved.

"I'll see you later. I want to soak in a hot tub to help soothe my jangling nerves."

Attractive as a lazy soak sounded, Lucy made do with a quick shower. Even though her appearance wasn't important, Lucy still took pains with her dressing. She smoothed makeup on with an expert hand, using eye shadow to deepen and enlarge her soft brown eyes. The scattering of freckles on her straight nose were softened by a discreet coating of powder, and her generous mouth was accented with clear red lip gloss. She arranged her hair in a sophisticated chignon, a style that emphasized the purity of her creamy skin as well as the graceful line of her neck. The dress she finally chose was an old favorite, an aquamarine silk with a halter top and a full, swirling skirt. Simple, yet elegant.

Briefly, Lucy wondered how this evening was going to work out. She had half-expected Caleb to make some kind of excuse when she'd invited him, but he hadn't. Neither had he made any attempt to contact her again.

The doorbell chimed at six forty-five and Lucy hurried to answer it, expecting her ex-husband. For some reason, despite his vague air and forgetful manner, he was never late to anything.

She swung the door open and blinked at the sight of Caleb Bannister. He looked as different from the scantily clad runner of last week as it was possible to look. His lean, muscled flesh was covered with an impeccably tailored three-piece light-gray suit. His flawless white shirt was set off by an oxford striped tie. Lucy was certain that his gleaming black leather shoes were handmade.

"Hello," Lucy mumbled, shocked at the wave of pleasure that engulfed her at the sight of him. "Hi," she repeated, getting a firm grip on herself. "Come in. I'm glad you could make it."

"My pleasure," he replied conventionally, and then handed her a large box of chocolates covered with gold foil.

Lucy's eyes gleamed with frank greed as she recognized the lady adorning them. The brand was her favorite, but owing to the price they were a treat reserved for special occasions.

"Thank you." She smiled at him and, unable to resist, promptly opened the box and, after he declined, ate one. "I *love* them," she confessed, as a bit of soft cherry cream caught on her lip.

"I thought of you when I saw the naked lady on the box," he said wickedly, grinning at her discomfort. He reached out and wiped the dripping sweet from her mouth with one long finger, then licked it clean.

Lucy shivered at the intimacy of the small act, but she forced her mind to concentrate on other things. She set the candy box down on the coffee table so that the other guests could have some, then turned to Caleb.

"May I get you a drink?" She caught herself just in time before offering him a whiskey. It was very awkward, knowing as much as she did about his personal habits, yet having to pretend that he was a virtual stranger. In some ways—and to Lucy it seemed to have nothing to do with her program—she felt she'd known him all her life. Maybe in another life, she thought fancifully. Caleb Bannister would have been a prime candidate for a lover from her distant past. Lucy shivered. She wasn't a fanciful person. Usually she dealt in facts and figures but there was something about Caleb Bannister that touched an unexpectedly responsive cord deep within her.

"Whiskey." He requested his usual before-dinner drink,

and Lucy, as if released from a spell, poured it for him. She also poured herself a glass of chilled white wine, more to have something to do with her hands than from any desire for a drink.

Lucy sank down on the sofa and watched as Caleb chose to sit beside her.

"I like your decorating scheme." He glanced with approval at the clean, uncluttered lines of her furniture.

"Thank you. I've enjoyed decorating the apartment"—she looked around the room—"but actually I'm far from finished. I intend to replace several of the more modern pieces with antiques. The trick is finding the piece you want at a price you can afford. But there's no hurry." She suddenly recalled how terribly wealthy Caleb was, and realized he never spoke of it.

Caleb leaned back against the sofa cushions and studied her. "You aren't planning on remarrying?" he asked idly.

"I've already tried marriage," Lucy said dryly, "and believe me, it isn't all it's cracked up to be."

"Just because you were hurt once—" he began.

"But I wasn't hurt," she corrected him. "Bored out of my skull, perhaps, but nothing so active as hurt. Why are you pushing marriage? You've never tried it."

"How do you know?" He eyed her narrowly.

Damn! Another bit of information she wasn't supposed to know yet.

"Because you have such an untrammeled look about you," she lied. "Nothing about you suggests domestic upsets and two-A.M. feedings."

"That's a myth."

"What is?" Lucy blinked, not following him.

"Two-A.M. feedings. My father's second wife had a baby when I was sixteen, and it screamed not only at two but at twelve, one, three, and four. That kid was a live advertisement for birth control. With Leslie behind me it's no wonder I never had the nerve to marry."

"Poor little devil." Lucy smiled, then felt a flash of

unease. There hadn't been any mention of a sister in any of Beth's copious notes. It made her wonder what other important facts had been left out. She was about to ask him casually about Leslie when, to her absolute amazement, he reached over and picked up her skirt, baring her slender legs.

She gasped. "What are you doing?"

"Don't panic. I simply want to check on your knees." He ran his finger lightly over her silk-clad skin. "Nice," he remarked, observing the few remaining scabs with satisfaction. "You have good healing skin."

"I also have a normal share of modesty," she muttered, pulling down her skirt. The touch of his fingers on her legs had been highly erotic. Her senses reeled even as she tried to get a grip on herself.

"You have a beautiful body, Lucy," he replied in a low voice.

"There's no reason to flaunt it," she said tartly.

"Nonsense, once we get you in shape—"

"In shape!" Lucy was outraged that he was back to that again. "What's wrong with my shape?"

"Nothing," he replied patiently. "I just told you that. Outwardly you look fine, but inwardly you sound like a car running on two cylinders the moment you start to run."

About to hotly deny any desire to engage in any activity more strenuous than sprinting for the bus, Lucy remembered Beth and swallowed her words. If he was serious about helping her set up a jogging program, then she could bring Beth along and further their plan. Of course, there was also the distinct possibility that once Caleb saw Beth tonight he'd forget all about wanting to help Lucy. The thought was vaguely depressing, and Lucy was glad when the doorbell rang, forcing her into the role of hostess.

CHAPTER
Four

BETH WAS STANDING in the hall beside Marcus, but her ex-husband's presence barely registered with Lucy. Her eyes widened at the picture Beth presented. Beth had said her dress would be sexy, but that was much too mild an assessment. Spectacular was more like it.

The gown's ultrathin straps served no useful purpose other than to emphasize the extreme frailty of Beth's fine-boned shoulders and satiny skin. The black lace bodice barely skimmed the tips of Beth's small, firm breasts, the fabric's ebony darkness highlighting their creamy perfection. The full chiffon skirt billowed out from her tiny waist, reaching to midcalf length. Pure silk stockings caressed the slender length of Beth's legs, while the few straps of black leather attached to the four-inch heels which passed for sandals called attention to her dainty feet.

It was a devastating outfit that would have raised the blood pressure of a confirmed misogynist. What it would do to a man who was already partial to blondes in black lace remained to be seen. Firmly stifling an unworthy impulse to slam the door on her friend, Lucy forced herself to smile welcomingly.

"You look lovely, Beth," she said honestly. "Absolutely gorgeous."

"Thank you." Beth gave a nervous giggle and glanced around Lucy. "Is he here yet?" she mouthed.

Lucy nodded, then smiled at her ex-husband. "Thanks for the things you brought by this afternoon, Marcus.

It's good to see you again." She ushered them into the living room.

"My pleasure, Lucy." Marcus absently dropped a kiss on her cheek.

Lucy glanced toward Caleb to find him studying them intently. A feeling of loss swept over her as she caught the momentary flash of predatory interest in his face before he smiled politely at the newcomers.

Score one for the computer. Lucy gave credit where it was due. The blonde in black lace had well and truly caught his attention.

"Beth, may I present Caleb Bannister. Caleb, Beth, my neighbor and good friend. And this is Marcus Blackmore."

"Beth." Bannister smiled politely at Beth, then turned to Marcus.

Marcus transferred the white plastic box he was carrying to his left hand and shook Caleb's outstretched hand.

"Say, Lucy"—Marcus motioned to the box—"this really should be refrigerated. Do you mind?"

"That depends," Lucy replied with a cautiousness learned from bitter experience. "What's in it and what does it smell like?"

"Why, Lucy!" Beth seemed surprised at her question. "I'll bet it's a corsage. Isn't it?" She glanced questioningly at Marcus.

"No," he replied. "It's a mouse I'm going to do some tissue cultures on later."

"You mean it's *dead?*" Beth stepped backward and looked uncertainly at Lucy, who couldn't resist a grin. Leave it to Marcus to bring a dead rodent to a dinner party.

"You mean you killed the poor thing?" Beth peeped at Caleb to see how he was reacting to her feminine ploy.

"Not exactly," Marcus replied seriously. "However, I did inject it with the cancer cells which eventually killed it. You may not realize it, but we can learn quite a bit about human cancers from studying animal tumors."

"I'll store it, as long as you guarantee that it won't leak the smell of formaldehyde all over my refrigerator," Lucy stipulated, remembering an earlier disaster.

"I quick-froze it." Marcus handed the box to Lucy, who gingerly accepted it. Intellectually she was well aware of the necessity of using mice for cancer experiments, but emotionally her sympathies were all with the animals.

"What branch of research are you in, Dr. Blackmore?" Caleb asked.

"Call me Marcus, please." Taking Caleb's arm, Marcus guided him into the living room as he began a technical discourse on his latest project.

Beth glanced at the engrossed men and followed Lucy into the tiny kitchen.

"It's stuffy in here," Beth said.

Lucy, rummaging through a drawer looking for plastic bags, answered, "I think it's just the heat from the cooking." She took the precaution of wrapping the box in three separate plastic bags before hiding it behind the lettuce in the vegetable crisper.

"Bannister's rather intimidating close up, isn't he?" Beth commented nervously.

"It's just his size." Lucy checked the rib roast. "He's not really intimidating."

"Nor smitten." Beth frowned. "He was so polite."

"What'd you expect? For him to grab you and begin to make mad, passionate love to you in front of us? Don't worry. I saw his face when I brought you into the room." Lucy forced herself to be honest. "He was interested, all right. And why shouldn't he be? You fulfill all his requirements—and in that dress you look like the stuff of which fantasies are made."

"As long as I'm the stuff of which marriages are made!" Beth laughed. "But, you know, your Marcus is kind of nice."

"First of all, he isn't my Marcus. And secondly, if

you've got a brain in your head, you'll stay away from him. Who needs a husband who brings home dead mice?"

"True." Beth shivered.

"Now, come on. Let's go break up their discussion. Once Marcus gets going on his research, he'll never stop. Besides, the whole purpose of this evening is to expose you to Bannister, and you aren't going to get much exposure hiding in my kitchen."

"I'm nervous," Beth whispered.

"There's no need to be," Lucy answered, trying to bolster her friend's sagging self-confidence. "All we're trying to do tonight is bait the trap. We've no need to rush things. You go on out. I'll be along in a minute."

"Okay." Beth obediently left while Lucy stared blankly at her colorful ceramic-tiled counter and tried to analyze her reluctance to think of Beth and Caleb as a couple.

Lucy was drawn to Caleb. Despite the brevity of their acquaintance, she felt a rapport with him. He was a kindred spirit in a world made up mainly of bland, innocuous personalities. But there was more to it than that. Lucy absently picked up a lettuce leaf and began to munch it.

Face it, she mused, forcing herself to put her feelings into coherent thoughts. You're sexually attracted to the man. Caleb Bannister emitted sexual vibrations that drew her like a bee to honey. Never before in her life had she fantasized about what it would be like to have a particular man make love to her, but she did with Caleb. She found herself daydreaming about him, an adolescent trait that she thought she'd outgrown ten years ago. And might as well have, for all the good it was going to do her. She hadn't really needed the computer to tell her that Caleb Bannister wasn't drawn to her type. He'd managed to communicate that very effectively himself. Men who were attracted to a woman didn't treat her like one of the guys, nor compare her to a dog, nor offer to teach her to jog. At least, the sophisticated type like Caleb Bannister didn't.

So where did that leave her? Lucy fished a radish out of the salad and began nibbling on it as she considered the question. But before she could come up with an answer, the doorbell rang again and she hastily went to answer it.

"Good evening." Lucy smiled warmly at the three new arrivals, then frowned slightly as she glanced around. "What happened to John?" she asked, fearing that her numbers were about to be upset again.

"He's parking the car." Linda gave a haughty toss of her fashionable mane of long brown curls. "Maybe I'll get lucky and he'll lock himself in."

"Oh?" Lucy shot a questioning glance at Jane and Tom Glasson, who were standing beside Linda.

Jane shrugged her plump shoulders as if to disclaim all knowledge of Linda's petulant mood.

It was obvious that Linda and her boyfriend had had a fight of impressive magnitude. Lucy only hoped that they would be polite enough at least to maintain some semblance of good manners toward each other, but she had her doubts. One of Linda's charms—or faults, depending on your point of view—was her tendency to say exactly what she thought with no regard for the social niceties of the situation.

Lucy winced inwardly. Things were becoming more complex by the minute.

"Let me introduce you to the rest of the guests," she said, closing the door behind them. "I imagine you have quite a bit in common with one of them, Tom. Caleb Bannister is in finance, too."

"*The* Caleb Bannister!" Tom shot a quick look into the living room. His eyes gleamed as they lit on Caleb, who was listening intently to whatever Marcus was saying, while Beth sat across from them trying to look interested.

Linda's eyes took on a gleam, too, as she sized Caleb up. She ran a slender hand down the silky red sheath she was wearing, moistened her lips in anticipation, and glided into the living room, her hips swaying provocatively.

Lucy firmly repressed an impulse to grab Linda by her avant-garde hairdo and demand that she leave Caleb Bannister alone. It was bad enough that Lucy had to help Beth charm him, but to have to watch Linda try her hand at it as well was asking too much.

"I wonder if this means she and John are breaking up," Jane said aloud, voicing the question in Lucy's mind.

"Who cares!" Tom snorted. "Do you know who that is? Caleb Bannister is one of *the* powers on the financial scene. Knowing him could do my career a great deal of good."

Lucy felt a momentary flash of anger at Tom's self-serving attitude, an anger she realized was totally unreasonable since she'd specifically invited him so that he could talk finance with Bannister.

"Lead on, fair Amazon," Tom quipped in a voice which carried into the living room. Caleb looked impassively at Tom and gave Lucy a curiously penetrating stare.

Hastily, Lucy rearranged her face into the semblance of a smile, as if amused by Tom's reference to her size. She'd learned long ago to act unconcerned at taunts about her height. If she didn't, they only got worse. Not that Tom was taunting her, she told herself. He'd been making cracks about her size since she'd met him six years ago. He was merely an insensitive clod.

By the time Lucy had performed the introductions, John had arrived. It was immediately obvious that he was in no better humor than Linda. He grunted a hello at the assembled company, glanced at Linda, then perched on the arm of the sofa next to her. She ignored him, concentrating the full battery of her sultry brown eyes on Bannister.

Lucy began to serve drinks while she tried to decide what to do about the latest unexpected turn of events.

She glanced questioningly at Beth, who merely looked back helplessly.

Lucy dropped the last ice cube into Jane's diet soda, handed it to her, then picked up the empty ice bucket. "I'll be back with more ice in a minute," she said.

"I'll help you, Lucy." Caleb stood up.

"Oh, but . . ." She blinked in confusion as he took the ice bucket out of her hands.

"I'll come, too." Linda started to rise.

"There's no need. Lucy and I can take care of it." Caleb's polite words had Linda sinking down onto the sofa again. If ever a tone of voice had indicated absolute lack of interest, Caleb's had. It was suddenly apparent to Lucy that he was quite capable of ruthlessness.

She followed meekly along behind him into the kitchen, uncertain about what had brought about his desire to accompany her.

"You didn't have to help," she offered tentatively as he opened the freezer and took out several trays of ice cubes.

"Actually, I was hoping you'd give me a score card." He deftly twisted the trays of ice into the bucket.

"A score card?" Lucy picked up a dish cloth and began wiping up the splinters of ice that had fallen onto the countertop.

"For that crew in there." He set the lid on the bucket and leaned back against the cabinets.

Lucy closed her eyes briefly as the faint spicy scent of his after shave teased her nostrils and drifted down to her lungs to constrict her breathing. As close as she was, the heat from his body enveloped her, and she was horrified at her almost overwhelming impulse to reach out and touch him.

"Score card?" she repeated bemusedly.

"Snap out of it, woman." Caleb unwittingly made the situation worse when one of his large hands closed over the nape of her neck and gave her a gentle shake. It was a lazy, assured gesture that hinted at his strength and made her feel small and helplessly feminine. Her heart began beating overtime, and she stiffened, afraid that he'd notice her involuntary reaction. It was imperative that he not realize she saw him as an attractive male.

"What do you want to know about them?" she asked.

"You're tense as a board," he marveled. He leaned back against the counter and pulled her unresisting body forward until she was leaning against him. "Relax." He pushed her head into his neck and began to massage her shoulders. "Did you have a bad day?"

Lucy grabbed at the excuse he offered. "Frightful. The payroll system blew up for the umpteenth time." Her words ended on a sigh as his soothing hands moved down to her hips.

Knowing that she was making a mistake, but not strong enough to resist, Lucy relaxed, letting his body support her weight. The scratchy, smooth texture of his suit rubbed against her cheek and she closed her eyes, blissfully reveling in the intoxicating feel of his hard body against her softness. This close, the smell of his after shave was stronger and mixed with several other elusive scents, all overlaid by the primitive, musky odor of the man himself.

"Poor Lucy. You ought to be in bed instead of entertaining."

Her heart stopped, then began racing as she was unable to suppress the images that flooded her mind at his words. Images of his massive body lying naked next to hers in the huge canopied bed in his room. Images of him bending over her, of his long fingers caressing her body. Horrified, Lucy clamped down on her wayward imagination, appalled at her uncharacteristic thoughts. She was behaving like a lovesick adolescent.

"So tell me"—Bannister's voice recalled her—"who are all those people?"

"Well..." Lucy tried to decide how much to tell him. "Tom is in banking."

"That much I know," he replied dryly. "I've never

gotten such a hard sell over cocktails in my life. He's also not very perceptive."

"Why?"

"You don't even remotely resemble an Amazon. They were superbly conditioned warriors."

"Thanks!" Lucy snapped, beginning to feel like she'd never live down her lack of athletic prowess.

"And you aren't the least bit ferocious," he continued. "As a matter of fact, I get the feeling that underneath your rather competent exterior, you're a soft touch."

"Oh?" Lucy looked up into his bright blue eyes. He was getting a little too close to the truth for comfort.

"And who are Mata Hari and Heathcliff?"

Lucy giggled at his apt description of them.

"Hmm, that feels good." Caleb grinned down at her.

"What does?"

"The feel of your body against mine when you laugh."

His words shook Lucy out of the sensual trap he was exerting, and she took a hasty step backward, making a show of checking the roast while she returned to his question. "Linda and John are, for want of a better term, live-in lovers. Normally you couldn't ask for two nicer people, but they seem to have quarreled."

"And she's trying to use me to make him jealous. Why doesn't she try Marcus?"

"Because John knows Marcus," Lucy replied, "and the only way Marcus would be interested in Linda would be if she were to suddenly sprout whiskers, white fur, and a long pink tail."

"You know Marcus, too, don't you?" Caleb's eyes narrowed as he watched Lucy's expressive face.

"If you want information, ask!" Lucy snapped. "There's no need to beat around the bush. It's certainly no secret. Marcus and I were married for five years."

"And you're still friends?"

"Why not?" Lucy shrugged. "We grew up together. Marcus is like a brother. I'll always be fond of him."

"Does that mean you're hoping for a reconciliation?"

"There is a vast difference between love and fondness!" Lucy said tartly. "Simply because I was too naive at eighteen to know that doesn't mean that I haven't learned it since. Besides"—she chuckled—"Marcus is no more eager to reestablish our former relationship than I am."

Lucy waited for him to ask about the last member of the dinner party—the one who, according to her program, should have been the embodiment of all his dreams. But he didn't, and she wondered why. Was he so impressed with Beth's physical attributes that he had no need to ask any questions? Was he prepared to accept her no matter what she was like? She was about to bring Beth's name up herself and try to gauge his reaction when Beth opened the door and entered.

Beth shot a shy, nervous smile at Caleb and spoke to Lucy. "I turned the air conditioning up again, Lucy. It's getting hotter out there."

"Thanks, Beth," she said, smiling at her nervous friend. "Why don't you take Caleb back into the living room while I get ready to serve dinner?" She forced herself to further Beth's cause even though she would rather have kept Caleb in the kitchen with her.

Lucy watched Beth link one slim, bare arm through Caleb's.

"Excellent idea, Lucy," cooed Beth, "I'm starved."

"Me too." Caleb gave Lucy an intimate smile that seemed to Lucy's bemused senses to hint at all kinds of things.

"Poor man." Beth patted his hand and gasped, seemingly overcome at her daring in touching him. "Come along. The sooner we leave Lucy alone, the sooner we'll get to eat."

"Too true," Lucy agreed, turning back to her hollandaise sauce, trying to ignore them as they left. But Caleb's image refused to be banished. She could still feel the imprint of his hard body where she'd been pressed up against him. Her breasts felt swollen and tight, and her stomach was a twisted mass of nerves. There was no doubt about it: all he had to do was to touch her to provoke a powerful reaction. One that was not reciprocated, Lucy acknowledged with brutal honesty. She already knew what it took to elicit a sexual response from Caleb Bannister, and she didn't have it—not by eight inches and about fifty pounds.

Lucy gave the hollandaise a last stir and began to transfer the food to the dining room. It might be less wearing on her nerves to continue to hide in the kitchen, but she owed it to Beth to try to move things along. The dinner party was turning out to be awkward enough without Lucy shirking her duties. Beth, for all her inventive ideas on trapping the unwary male, had almost no concept of how to play hostess—and Emily Post herself, Lucy thought wryly, would have found it hard to keep this dinner party on an even keel.

For a while it looked as if things might improve. Lucy sat Marcus and Linda on either side of her at the foot of the table, putting Jane and Beth beside Caleb at the other end and leaving John and Tom in the middle. She could count on Jane to be polite without being flirtatious, which should have left the field open for Beth to shine. Unfortunately, it very quickly became obvious that Lucy's careful plans were doomed from the start. Jane behaved according to plan, but to Lucy's dismay no one else did. Beth failed to take advantage of her position and sat silently eating, speaking only when spoken to.

Linda, apparently spurred to greater efforts by Caleb's earlier lack of interest, flirted outrageously with him down the length of the table. John totally ignored his social obligations in favor of glaring furiously at Linda, while Tom continued to try to interest Caleb in some scheme or other that his bank was promoting. Marcus, instead of keeping Linda occupied, simply ignored everyone and ate with the singleminded concentration of imminent starvation.

Halfway through the main course, Lucy caught Caleb's eye and almost choked at the look of unholy glee he sent her. So much for her hope that she was exaggerating the problem in her own mind. God only knew what Caleb really thought about this motley assortment of guests or the hostess who'd assembled them.

The dinner ground its way down to dessert while Lucy despaired of ever improving the situation. There were simply too many people, each with his or her own ax to grind. Not that it really mattered. All that had been lost was her reputation as a hostess, and that wasn't really important. The main purpose of the evening had been to expose Beth to Caleb, and that had certainly been a success. Lucy remembered his arrested look when he'd caught sight of Beth for the first time. Surreptitiously, Lucy wiggled in her chair. She felt hot and stifled.

Jane caught Lucy's movement and fanned herself with her napkin. "Lucy, is it my imagination, or is it hot in here?"

"I thought it was just me." Lucy frowned as she remembered the problems she'd had earlier with the air conditioning. She rose and checked the temperature, wincing at the ninety degrees it registered. "It definitely isn't you, Jane." She tried turning the control all the way down, but the unit refused to switch on.

"Try hitting it," Linda suggested, and Lucy did, simply because she had no other ideas.

"Well, what happened?" Linda demanded.

"I hurt my hand," Lucy said with a grimace. "I think I'd better call the superintendent."

A short phone call was sufficient to find out that the problem was confined to the four apartments on her side of the hallway. Moreover, the maintenance man had not been encouraging about exactly when it would be fixed. His vague assurances about getting someone out first thing in the morning were none too comforting. She could suffocate by morning, Lucy thought indignantly, since none of the windows in her nineteenth-floor apartment opened.

"Why don't you allow me to take all of you out to a nightclub to round out the evening?" Caleb offered unexpectedly.

"We'd love to," Linda and Tom replied simultaneously, while John, if possible, looked even madder.

Lucy looked at Beth, who was nodding emphatically, and she sighed inwardly. Much as she welcomed the opportunity to prolong her time in Caleb's company, the thought of trying to continue to cope with this ill-assorted group squelched her enthusiasm.

"I'll have to decline," Marcus spoke up. "I have to do some tissue cultures on that mouse tonight. It was a lovely dinner, Lucy." He looked regretfully at the leftover food.

Familiar with his habit of subsisting on fast food, Lucy had no trouble correctly interpreting his unspoken plea.

"Wait a minute before you go, Marcus, and I'll wrap up some leftovers for you to take home with you." Lucy smiled at him.

Looking happy to have solved his eating problems for the weekend, Marcus wandered into the living room and sat down to munch chocolates while he waited for Lucy to pack his food.

Fifteen minutes later, she found herself sandwiched in between Beth and Caleb in the front seat of his silver Mercedes as they sped across town to meet the rest of the party at the nightclub.

CHAPTER
Five

Lucy stifled a gasp as she stepped into the reception room of the exclusive Alhambra Club. In keeping with its Arabian name, it boasted a Moorish theme. Hundreds of yards of purple silk had been draped from the ceiling to create the illusion of being in an opulent tent. A magnificent leaded antique oil lamp hung on a long silver chain over the ornately laquered reception desk. Several colorful Kharman rugs were scattered across the highly polished black marble floor.

The main room of the club had been decorated to resemble an Eastern garden. A huge fountain splashed in the center of the room, and hundreds of potted palms had been arranged to create walkways and secluded alcoves where patrons could relax in relative isolation if their tastes ran toward privacy.

Immediately to the right of the entrance was a cloak room, attended by a gorgeous brunette dressed in a minuscule top of purple satin heavily encrusted with gold sequins, and a brief bikini bottom overlaid with chiffon harem legs. The woman's eyes glowed with predatory interest at the sight of Caleb, and Lucy felt an involuntary flash of anger.

"There they are!" Beth's tug on her arm provided a welcome distraction from the unexpected stab of jealousy, which Lucy didn't want to even acknowledge, let alone explore.

Lucy forced her eyes away from Caleb—who was leaving Beth's lace shawl with the delighted brunette—

and looked across the room. The Glassons and Linda and John were seated on an ornately gilded bench, looking rather bemused by their surroundings.

Lucy waved, and the group hurried over to her.

"Isn't this fabulous?" Jane whispered. "Have you seen...?" she nodded toward the hat-check girl, who was making a big production out of giving Caleb his claim check. Not that he seemed to be objecting, Lucy noticed sourly, giving him a frosty look once he finally managed to tear himself away. Really, she thought, men were so stupid. They fell for the most obvious ploys. Turning her back on him, she totally missed the gleam of humor that momentarily lit his brilliant blue eyes.

The sight of Caleb Bannister galvanized the supercilious maître d' into immediate action. They were welcomed with a reverence that Lucy found rather amusing and Caleb himself ignored. It was obvious that he was a valued client, and she wondered which of the petite blondes in the computer's data banks he'd been in the habit of bringing here. Probably all of them, judging from the warmth of his welcome.

"Lucy," Beth whispered as they trailed along behind their host, "are you all right? You look sort of pained."

"I was just thinking about my air conditioning," she lied. There was no reason for her to spoil Beth's evening simply because she couldn't seem to get a handle on her wayward feelings. It was totally unlike her to be jealous, and Caleb wasn't even her escort. He was Beth's. Her "date" was home eating her leftovers and looking at tissue cultures.

The maître d' seated them around a table on the edge of the dance floor, directly across from the band. Linda, moving fast, grabbed hold of Caleb's arm and slipped into the seat to his left. Beth managed to appropriate the chair on his right, barely beating out Tom, who apparently hadn't finished his sales pitch yet. Lucy fought down an impulse to laugh at the whole situation. The only women not fighting for Caleb Bannister's attention were Jane, who was clearly overawed by her surroundings, and Lucy herself, who knew only too well the futility of trying to compete.

Lucy sagged into the red leather seat and slipped off her shoes, gratefully resting her aching feet on the cool marble floor. She sighed in blissful comfort and glanced up, her gaze becoming entrapped in Caleb's as he focused on her mouth. His look seemed to caress her lips.

He probably doesn't even see you, she told herself. The waitress provided a distraction, and she turned gratefully at the sound of her voice.

A clone of the hat-check girl stood by their table, giving Caleb a dazzling smile. Lucy ordered a margarita when her turn came.

"She'd make a great belly dancer," Jane said, eyeing the scantily clad waitress as she glided away.

"She's too thin," Lucy responded. "Besides, belly dancing is an art form that takes years to learn."

"Really?" Jane looked interested.

"It's true." Beth giggled. "Lucy and I signed up for lessons at the Y two years ago. They were taught by this Syrian lady who must have tipped the scales at two hundred pounds. She took one look at me and said I was much too skinny. But Lucy . . ." Beth giggled again. "She said Lucy had the talent to make the Osmans themselves stand up and take notice."

Linda looked confused. "Donny and Marie?"

"No—Osmans as in the sultans," Lucy enlightened her. "You remember Selim, Bajazet, Suleiman, that lot."

"Their tastes ran toward Amazons?" Tom asked in a heavyhanded attempt at humor.

"Must have." Lucy tried to keep the irritation out of her voice. For some reason, Tom's wisecracks were especially bothering her tonight. Maybe, she admitted to herself, she just didn't want Caleb to be endlessly reminded that she did not meet his specifications.

"The band sounds heavenly," Linda said pointedly, throwing a come-hither look at Caleb that promised all kinds of things.

"Yes, it does," he agreed. "Lucy, would you like to dance?"

"But..." Linda began.

"Lucy is, after all, our hostess this evening," he explained, unwittingly ruining her enjoyment of his invitation. Even so, she had no intention of refusing.

"I'd love to," Lucy accepted, jamming her protesting feet back into her shoes.

"Come on, Tom, let's dance too." Jane pulled her husband out onto the floor, leaving Beth alone with the sulking Linda and the furious John.

Lucy felt guilty at abandoning Beth, but she ignored it. She'd put up with all kinds of horrors in the course of Beth's pursuit of a husband. It wouldn't hurt Beth to suffer a little, too.

They reached the minuscule dance floor as the band began to play a slow, dreamy tune. Caleb pulled Lucy close, fitting her body to the long length of his.

"Put your arms around my waist," he ordered as one large hand held her head against his shoulder. She obeyed, snuggling close to him and absorbing the myriad sensations caused by the movement of his body against hers. She blanked out the rational voice in the back of her mind that warned her that she was playing with fire, and simply enjoyed the feelings.

Someone jostled her from behind, and Caleb's arms pulled her even closer, making it physically impossible for them to do more than merely sway in place. Nervously, Lucy stiffened. She glanced around, but there was nothing unusual about the way he was holding her. Most of the couples were dancing in a similar manner.

"Relax, woman." Caleb's left hand gently massaged her back, sending her heartbeat skyrocketing and making relaxation the furthest thing from her mind. "We'll entertain them for a couple of hours, and then you can go home and get some rest—provided that John doesn't break up the party first by strangling Linda."

"I doubt that anyone would care at this point," Lucy said tartly. "Besides, I can't really blame John, even if he is overreacting. It's unforgivable of Linda to involve a third party in a personal fight."

"Do they do this kind of thing often?" Caleb asked curiously.

"Hardly, or I'd never have invited them. I've known them for almost four years, and this is the first time I've ever been caught in the fallout."

"They've been living together for four years?"

"At least." Lucy glanced curiously at him, surprised at the faint sound of disapproval in his voice. In the information she'd fed into the computer there had been no mention of a woman ever actually living with him. "You don't approve?"

"I'm a lawyer, and lawyers hate loose ends. Believe me, living together can create some monstrous complications, especially if there are kids or property involved. But enough of those two." He gently pushed her cheek against his neck.

Lucy moved her head ever so slightly, reveling in the faintly scratchy feel of his jawline. That close to him, she could see the blond shadow on his face. He must have a heavy beard, she realized in surprise. Caleb would have to shave again at night before he made love. The idle thought flitted through her mind, making her miss a step when she realized where her thoughts were leading.

She peeped up at Caleb and her feet became entangled entirely as he gave her a slow, knowing grin that seemed to read her mind. Fortunately for her self-possession, the music stopped and she was able to escape the sensual trap of his arms. She needed time to think, to sort out her uncharacteristic thoughts and redirect them along more acceptable avenues. She tried to convince herself that Caleb Bannister was a virtual stranger to her, but it wasn't exactly true.

"Lucy"—Caleb touched her arm as they moved off the dance floor—"what's wrong?" He stared down into her bleak face.

"Nothing." She forced a light laugh. "Just my tired feet."

He frowned, obviously unconvinced, but before he could pursue the matter, Linda stood up and grabbed his arm, dragging him back toward the dance floor. Short of causing a scene, there was little he could do about it.

Lucy sank down into her seat and drained the remains of her drink. She signaled the waitress for another and asked Beth, "Where's John?"

"In the men's room." Beth sighed. "And I hope he stays there. He's behaving like a perfect idiot."

"Who isn't?" Lucy snapped, thinking of her own foolish reaction to Caleb.

"Are you all right, Lucy?" Beth looked concerned at her friend's acerbic tone. "Bannister wasn't nasty to you, was he?"

"Good Lord, no!" Lucy blinked in surprise. "Why would you think that?"

"I'm not sure." Beth grimaced. "Probably because I can't seem to tell when he's serious and when he's joking."

"Does that mean you're having second thoughts about your plan?" Lucy asked, unsure of whether she was pleased or not. On the one hand it would be nice not to have to try to push Beth at Caleb. But then again, if Beth pulled out of the running, there would be no excuse for Lucy herself to see him.

"No." Beth's pretty little face set in mulish lines.

Lucy attributed her relief to her professional desire to see her computer application through to its logical conclusion, refusing to look any deeper than that.

"I'm not going to quit!" Beth insisted. "I've worked too hard on this. I just need a little more time."

"If you say so." Lucy accepted her second drink from the waitress and began to absently lick the salt from the rim of the glass as her eyes automatically searched the crowded dance floor for Linda and Caleb.

They weren't hard to find. Linda's red dress showed clearly against the somber hue of Caleb's suit. Lucy forced herself to watch them dispassionately. It was impossible to draw any conclusions from studying his face— it was a polite social mask, charming, attentive, and completely bland. Neither was there anything to be discovered by watching them dance, although it was apparent from the faintly dissatisfied look on Linda's face that she didn't like the slight space he was maintaining between their bodies. A space that was as much mental as physical, Lucy realized with a start as she inadvertently caught Caleb's eye and watched an expression of amused indulgence flit over his lean features. He was bored with the luscious Linda. Her obvious pursuit of him had left him cold.

"Lucy, are you listening to me?" Beth's plaintive voice cut the invisible thread that seemed to tie her to Caleb, and she thankfully turned back to her friend. If she wasn't careful, she was going to give Caleb the idea that she was interested in him—that she couldn't keep her eyes off him even when he had another woman in his arms. Not that it was true, she tried to convince herself. The only reason she was paying such close attention to him was to see if he was reacting according to her program.

The evening was showing all the signs of turning into a first-class disaster. Linda seemed determined to gain a response to her flirtations from Caleb—and from John. But John, now well beyond sullen glares, ignored her, choosing instead to drown his anger in a seemingly never-ending supply of Scotch. Linda flirted all the harder, taking every opportunity to run her long red nails over Caleb's arm.

Blood-red, Lucy thought with an inward shiver. She had ceased to feel even faintly jealous. Linda was being too obvious. The situation wasn't helped any by Tom's ham-fisted attempts at humor. Tom's latest contribution was to laughingly tell John he'd best watch out or Bannister would be stealing his girlfriend from him.

Lucy finished her third drink and considered ordering a fourth. So far the alcohol she'd consumed hadn't affected her at all, and what she really craved was something to slightly blur what was happening around her. She remembered hearing that perfectly rational people could act entirely out of character, depending on the actions of the individuals around them. For the first time Lucy truly understood group dynamics. Her normal, sane friends all seemed to have developed hitherto unsuspected personality traits—and she herself wasn't immune, she thought in disgust. Instead of attempting to solve the problem, she was trying to decide how much more liquor it would take to render her insensitive to the situation.

Even Beth didn't seem to be doing much to help her own cause, Lucy noticed with tired indifference. Other than a very occasional remark, she was virtually silent—unprecedented behavior for the volatile Beth.

Fortunately for Lucy's sobriety, Linda pushed John too far sooner rather than later. Beth was dancing with Tom, leaving an uneasy quintet at the table. Linda, after an abortive attempt to coerce Caleb into dancing with her again, picked up his hand, turned it over, and ran a fingernail across his large palm.

"Let me tell your fortune." Linda laughed, while Lucy definitely decided to have another drink. She hadn't heard anyone use that corny line as an excuse to touch someone since she'd been in high school.

"I see a new sex interest in your life." Linda gave another inane giggle, but before Caleb could respond, John finally reached flash point.

"I'll sex-interest you, you damned little flirt!" John slammed down the full glass of Scotch he'd been holding and jerked Linda away form Caleb. "And as for you!" John clenched his fist and glared at Bannister.

Oh, God, no! Lucy prayed. Caleb would never forgive her if her dinner party ended with a drunken brawl in a

public place. Not giving herself time to consider the
wisdom of her action, she leaned over, picked up John's
drink, and dumped the whole thing into his lap. If Lucy
had been in a mood to be amused, the expression on
John's face as the icy liquid penetrated the material of
his pants and ran down his legs would have sent her into
gales of laughter. But she wasn't. All she wanted to do
was to escape before John disgraced them all.

"So clumsy of me," she murmured to the stunned faces
around the table. "If you'll excuse me, I need to visit
the ladies' room." She beat a hasty retreat before anyone
could respond.

She rather expected one of the other women to come
after her, but no one did. She hung around the women's
lounge as long as she could, combing and recombing her
hair and retouching her makeup. Finally, the suspicious
glances the attendant was giving her penetrated, and with
a reluctant sigh she dropped a tip on the plate and left.
She had to face them sometime; it might as well be now.

To her surprise, Caleb was the only one at the table.
Lucy looked around to see if the others were dancing,
but they weren't. Nonchalantly she slid into her seat and
smiled uncertainly at him.

"Where is everyone?" she asked.

"Probably hiding. Tell me," he queried evenly, "do
you often do things like that?"

"No," Lucy answered honestly, "I simply wanted to
stop John before he did something I'd regret. And his
drink was just sitting there."

"I suppose he ought to be grateful that he wasn't
drinking hot coffee, since then it wouldn't have mattered
whether or not he made up his quarrel with Linda."

"They made it up?" Lucy asked, ignoring the impli-
cations of the rest of his comment.

"Uh-huh. Linda was oozing sympathy all over him as
he took her away."

"Good!"

"Do you really care?"

"Not at the moment," Lucy answered truthfully. "Right now I'm simply glad they've left. Where's everybody else?"

"After John limped out, supported by the repentant Linda, Jane discovered a headache and Tom decided to call it an evening."

"What! Without selling you whatever it was he was pushing?" Lucy laughed.

"I understand I'm to be given a second chance." Caleb chuckled. "Not that it'll do him any good. He'll never get past my secretary."

Lucy watched the look of distaste that flitted across his face at the mention of Tom's pushy tactics, and she remembered her earlier feeling about his ruthlessness. He'd suffered Tom's hard-sell technique tonight with stoic politeness, probably because of his status as a guest. But there was no doubt that Tom would be effectively excluded in the future. Would Caleb do the same to Lucy for having involved him in this social fiasco in the first place? The thought hung in her mind like a poison dart.

"And what are you thinking about to make you look so unhappy?" Caleb ran a gentle finger down her nose.

"General regret for the evening," Lucy blurted out, slightly unnerved by the warm flood of pleasure that shook her at his casual caress. "And to think that I invited Tom for you," Lucy added, trying to make a joke of it.

"When you know me better, you find that I never mix business with pleasure."

"Oh?" Lucy responded, uncertain what to say. Was he telling her that she was going to have a chance to get to know him better? Or was it an oblique warning that he intended to pursue Beth and so Lucy was bound to see him? It was impossible to try to guess his meaning, so she sensibly decided to wait and see what happened. Reminded of Beth, she quickly looked around again, ashamed that simply talking to Caleb could so quickly make her forget her friend.

"Where is Beth?" she demanded, rather as if she suspected him of hiding her somewhere.

"Tom and Jane offered to drop her off on their way home."

"They did?" Lucy frowned. "But why would they do that? Beth and I are both going to the same place. Why didn't they wait for me?"

"Perhaps they thought you were planning to spend the night in the ladies' lounge."

"Well, really," Lucy protested. "I wasn't gone *that* long."

"Thirty-five minutes."

"Oh," she replied blankly, remembering the strange stares the attendant had given her. No wonder the poor woman had been suspicious. "For heaven's sake, why didn't Beth come and get me?"

"Maybe she had fears for that gorgeous outfit she was wearing," he quipped, but Lucy barely heard the teasing tone. What did register was the very real admiration in his voice when he mentioned Beth's dress. Quite obviously he'd been impressed.

Lucy forced herself to champion her friend. "It certainly was a beautiful gown, but nowhere near as gorgeous as Beth herself."

"Unique, if your tastes run to petite green-eyed blondes with a soporific brand of chatter."

And yours do, Lucy slightly acknowledged, attributing her feelings of dejection to the lateness of the hour and the liquor she'd consumed.

"There you go again," Caleb said, watching her expression. "You wouldn't happen to be a weepy drunk, would you?"

"I wouldn't know!" Lucy replied haughtily. "I'm not in the habit of getting drunk. Furthermore, I'm not drunk now."

"I know, just tired." He grinned at her. "Come on. It's time to leave. This whole evening has been too much for you."

In more ways than one, she silently agreed as he

guided her across the crowded, noisy club.

Outside, a light rain was falling and Lucy gratefully turned up her hot face into the night. The gentle drops cooled her heated skin. She knew she should offer to go home in a taxi, but she was unable to bring herself to cut short the pleasure of these last few minutes alone with Caleb, especially since she didn't know when—or even if—she'd see him again. One thing was certain. If he wanted to court Beth, he would hardly be inclined to continually drag Lucy along as chaperone.

"You're going to get all wet." Caleb laughed as he watched Lucy stretch out her pink tongue to catch a raindrop.

"It's all right. I don't melt." Lucy laughed, too, suddenly feeling inordinately cheerful. She slipped into the soft leather seat of the Mercedes and sniffed appreciatively.

"What's the matter?"

"Nothing. I just love the smell of leather. It reminds me of fall, rustling leaves, and the first day of school."

"Why?"

"Because I always got a new pair of shoes then," Lucy explained patiently. "I used to love the first day of school, didn't you?"

"Not particularly. My parents couldn't agree on who should get custody of me, so they sent me to boarding school. Buckle up, Lucy."

"Okay." Lucy ineffectively fumbled with the strange-locking mechanism while she considered his words. There had been no mention of his parents' divorce in the data she'd fed into the computer—nor of his stepmother and younger half-sister, whom he'd mentioned earlier. She licked her lips uneasily. There were definitely some gaps in her program—gaps that could change the end result. It was possible that his parents' unhappy experience had permanently soured him on marriage, but she could hardly ask.

"Here." He gently removed her fumbling hands and, reaching across her, untangled the shoulder harness.

Lucy bit her lip as he leaned over her. A shiver slithered down her spine as his hand brushed negligently across her breast as he adjusted the strap. His blond hair gleamed silver in the dim light, and Lucy had the eerie sensation that she was looking forty years into the future, seeing what he'd look like when he was an old, old man. But she wouldn't be there, the devastating thought swept over her. Forty years from now he wouldn't even remember who Lucy Travers had been, while she had the unhappy premonition that his image would burn in her mind as clearly then as it did now. It was not a comforting thought.

CHAPTER
Six

"Lean back and close your eyes," Caleb ordered. "You look beat."

"Thanks." Lucy laughed. "You certainly have a way with words."

"There's no need for a lot of trite compliments between us," he said frankly.

"True," Lucy had no choice but to agree, "but on the other hand, you can carry the honesty bit too far. Remember what happened to Tolstoy."

"Tolstoy?" Caleb inserted a cassette into the tape deck, adjusting the volume downward as dreamy music flooded the car.

"I think it was Tolstoy." She snuggled down into the seat, letting the gentle music flow over her. "At any rate, it was one of those Russian authors."

"So what happened?" Caleb prompted.

"Well, it seemed that he and his new wife decided that the trouble with most marriages was a lack of honesty, so they pledged total candor. They started off their marriage with him telling her that her feet smelled, and she retaliated by informing him that his breath smelled. It was all downhill from there."

"No wonder." Caleb chuckled. "A person needs some illusions."

"Too true." Lucy relaxed, allowing herself to drift along with the soft music. Not quite asleep, but not quite awake either, she felt pleasantly suspended in between.

The car came to a quiet halt and Lucy tried to sit up, coming fully awake.

"Wake up, Lucy." Caleb ran a gentle finger down her straight nose before outlining her slightly parted lips. "Come on, sleepyhead." He released the seat belt and leaned across her to open the car door. "Try to stay awake long enough to get inside."

"I will," she answered petulantly. "I would hardly expect you to carry me."

"Don't assume I couldn't," he responded, helping her out of the car, "but, contrary to what the movies would have you believe, it's not that easy to grab a full-grown woman and go charging up a flight of stairs. It may look romantic, but take my word for it, the man is so winded by the time he gets to the top that he doesn't give a damn about romance."

"Did you ever try it?" Lucy asked curiously.

"In my impressionable youth." He chuckled. "During my senior year of college, I took some girl to see a movie in which the hero picked up the heroine and carried her up two flights of stairs before making passionate love to her. My apartment didn't have two flights of stairs, but it did have a freestanding wrought-iron spiral staircase leading up to the loft bedroom. So after we'd both had a drink, I gave my best Clark Gable imitation, lifted her into my arms, and charged up the stairs."

"Don't stop now! What happened?" Lucy demanded.

"I forgot to allow for the narrowness of the staircase. Her leg went through one of the rails, and when I tried to adjust for it, her head hit against the steps. She screamed, I overbalanced, and we wound up in a tangled heap at the bottom."

Lucy laughed, unable to stop herself at the thought of the sophisticated Caleb Bannister in such a predicament. "You poor soul," she managed to get out.

"She wasn't amused," he continued, "especially when she realized that I'd broken my arm and our whole weekend was going to have to be canceled. She stormed out in a huff, and I had to take a taxi to the emergency room of the local hospital. I felt like a damned fool trying to explain to the doctor how it had happened. He managed to keep a straight face, but the X-ray technician kept snickering in the background. The worst of it was that the girl was just a little bit of a thing."

His girlfriends always were, Lucy remembered with a pang.

She was about to say something when it suddenly struck her that they weren't anywhere near her apartment. She glanced around the darkened street. They seemed to be in some kind of an alley with garages on the left and huge homes on the right.

"Where are we?" she demanded.

"Home." He guided her up the shallow brick stairs.

"Yours?"

"Yep." He unlocked the back door and pushed it open.

Lucy allowed herself to be hustled inside before she protested. "Why did you bring me here?"

"What else was I supposed to do with you?" he asked. "You could hardly spend the night in a closed apartment with no air conditioning. It's probably over a hundred degrees in there by now. I suppose I could have taken you to a hotel, but you haven't any luggage. Besides, there's plenty of room here."

Lucy glanced around the dimly lit kitchen as she considered what he'd said. He was right about one thing. She certainly couldn't spend the night in her apartment. But she knew that Beth would be quite willing to let her sleep on her couch. All she had to do was ask. Lucy barely considered the idea before banishing it. Beth was her good friend and fellow conspirator, but there was no way Lucy was going to trade an evening in a gorgeous mansion for a lumpy couch—to say nothing of spending the time in such close proximity to Caleb.

Caleb closed the door and moved over to the kitchen counter.

Lucy shot him a covert glance. He began spooning

cocoa powder into two mugs. She watched as he stopped to slip off his jacket and toss it over the counter. His vest and tie followed. He certainly didn't look like a man bent on seduction, she admitted, ignoring the tiny pang of regret that the realization brought. If she had been Beth, he wouldn't be casually making cocoa, of all things. He'd probably be plying her with brandy.

Caleb poured boiling water into the mugs from a device on the sink and then set them on the Delft-tiled countertop. He opened the stainless-steel door of the biggest refrigerator Lucy had ever seen and peered inside. She winced at the sound of bottles being shoved about. Someone wasn't going to be too happy in the morning when they discovered the mess he'd made.

Lucy's curiosity got the better of her. "Who keeps the kitchen so clean for you?"

"Mrs. Woods." His voice came from the depths of the refrigerator. "She and her husband have an apartment on the lower level. They never come up after five unless I'm entertaining."

So that's what was behind the shutters, Lucy thought. It also explained why his house always seemed to be in such pristine condition.

"Ah!" Caleb grunted with satisfaction as he emerged from the refrigerator with a can of whipped cream. He gave it a vigorous shake and liberally squirted topping into one of the mugs. "Want some?" he questioned, his hand poised over the other.

Lucy nodded, watching in fascination as he generously piled her mug. He obviously had no need to watch his calories, Lucy thought wryly, and then wondered whether she should feel complimented or hurt that he wasn't watching hers. Dismissing the question as unprofitable, she took the mug he held out and licked the cream.

"Have a seat." He motioned toward the stools lining the breakfast bar.

Lucy hiked herself up, catching her breath as Caleb

sat down on the stool beside her. His wide shoulders were touching hers and he flashed her a companionable grin before taking a sip of his cocoa. Apparently her presence caused none of the prickles of awareness in him that his did in her.

"I must thank you for your invitation to dinner this evening," he said.

"Must you!" Lucy took exception to his choice of words.

"Don't go all prim and proper on me," he ordered. "I'm not in the mood for soothing injured feelings."

"Oh? What kind of mood are you in?"

Caleb shot her a sensual glance from his azure eyes and his mouth lifted in a slow, tantalizing grin.

Lucy's breathing quickened at the suggestive light in his eyes even as she firmly clamped down on her errant thoughts. It was obvious that he was merely teasing her. If he'd been serious, he could have easily engineered a more romantic setting. If he'd really wanted to make a pass at her, he'd hardly have seated her on a breakfast stool. He's have seated her on one of the sofas in the room where they'd had dinner last weekend. There he could have kissed her in comfort. Here he was liable to break his neck if he tried anything.

Lucy used the excuse of reaching for her cocoa to inch slightly away from contact with his hard body. She was tired and irritable, and she didn't need the added discomfort of one-sided sexual attraction.

"Tell me about Marcus." Caleb's question surprised her. She looked up at him, but his face told her nothing. He wore a calm, detached expression, looking rather like a doctor. Certainly he didn't seem overeager to know anything, but it wasn't the first time he'd asked about Marcus.

"Why?" she finally asked.

"Why not?" He shrugged his massive shoulders, bringing them into momentary contact with her again. "Yours has to be the most civilized split I've ever heard of, and I wondered why. Most of the divorces I've seen in the course of my career have been bitter affairs full of accusations and resentment."

"Have you ever handled a divorce?" Lucy asked, curious to know his feelings about the subject.

"Only once. My first year out of law school I helped a friend try to get custody of his kids."

"Did you win?"

"There were no winners," he said flatly. "My friend got custody, and his wife took an overdose of sleeping pills."

Lucy winced.

"I felt like I'd killed her. I knew she was unstable. That's why I agreed to break my own ban on divorce cases and help him. But I never expected her to kill herself."

Lucy put her hand over his clenched fist, her desire to comfort him overwhelming. "You can't accept responsibility for another person's actions," Lucy said seriously. "It's hard enough to take credit for your own."

Caleb returned the pressure of her hand and smiled tiredly. "Intellectually, I know you're right; but, emotionally, I can't quite reconcile myself to the fact."

Eager to banish the bleak look on his face, Lucy broke her long-standing rule never to discuss her marriage. "What do you want to know about Marcus?"

"Are you still in love with him?"

"Not exactly. I love Marcus, but I'm not *in* love with him. We've a whole lifetime of shared memories. I'll always be fond of him, but I don't love him the way a woman needs to love a man if they're going to have any hope of building a future together."

"Then why did you marry him?" Caleb asked reasonably.

"I was young," Lucy said simply. "Young and in love with love. I learned quickly that there's a whole lot more to marriage than a huge wedding and a honeymoon in the Bahamas. There are missed dinners, tensions over bills and work, all kinds of little irritants. In a sense love is the oil that keeps the marriage moving through all the little day-to-day annoyances. If you haven't got it, the little frictions will overwhelm you. Lord, listen to me!" Lucy laughed in embarrassment. "I sound like an advice-to-the-lovelorn column."

Uncertainly, she picked up her cocoa and sipped it. For some reason she didn't want to discuss her former marriage with Caleb. It made her very uncomfortable—and the cause wasn't simply her innate sense of privacy. It was more a desire to pretend that her abortive marriage had never occurred, a feeling she didn't understand. She'd never before felt the need to apologize for having been divorced.

"I don't know about advice to the lovelorn, but you certainly seem to have learned something from the experience. Have you any desire to marry again?"

It wasn't that easy, Lucy thought, remembering just how hard Beth was working to find a husband. She herself was operating under the additional handicap of being eight inches taller and three years older than Beth. But thinking of Beth reminded her of the program, and she felt obligated to do some probing of her own, even though her heart wasn't really in it. She dodged his question.

"What about you, Caleb? Why haven't you ever married?"

"Because I've never before found a woman I thought I could stand to live with for the rest of my life."

"Before?" Lucy picked up on the qualifying word.

"Uh-huh," he agreed, but he didn't elaborate—to Lucy's relief. She didn't want to hear him put his feelings for Beth into words.

"Finish your cocoa," he ordered with a glance at his wafer-thin gold watch. "It's almost two."

Lucy obediently gulped down the rest of her drink and slipped off the stool. She followed him out of the kitchen and up the back stairs to the second floor, where he opened the door directly across from the room where she'd used the bathroom on her first visit.

"This should do." He switched on the light and stepped aside for her to enter. Lucy looked around the spacious room in approval, even while common sense told her that the color scheme was highly impractical. A pale almond-colored carpet covered the floor and complemented matching almond-colored wallpaper, patterned with faint green leaves and tiny persimmon berries. A large chaise longue was upholstered in a matching material, which had also been used for the comforter on the full-sized canopied bed.

"It's absolutely gorgeous," Lucy replied honestly.

"There's a bath through there." He pointed to a door in the far wall. "Why don't you get ready and I'll find some pajamas for you? There should be a new toothbrush in the medicine cabinet. Help yourself."

"Thank you," Lucy said weakly. The thought of wearing Caleb's pajamas was doing strange things to her nerves.

The guest bathroom wasn't as impressive as the master bath, but it was certainly more elaborate than her own at home. Thick wall-to-wall carpeting covered the floor, and the same wallpaper as in the becroom decorated three of the walls. The fourth was entirely mirrored above a vanity with two sinks, which had the same green-leaf pattern painted on them. There was a large tub and a separate shower stall.

A quick shower made Lucy suddenly feel very sleepy, and she could barely keep her eyes open as she took a fresh toothbrush out of the medicine cabinet and cleaned her teeth.

Cautiously, she opened the bedroom door a crack and peered into the bedroom. She remembered Caleb's cheerful lack of concern about walking in on her when she'd been in the tub. To her relief, the door was closed and the room was empty. A jade-green pajama top tossed carelessly on the bed showed that he'd been there while she was showering.

Lucy slipped the top over her head and ran her hand down over the lustrous silk, reveling in the sensuous feel of the sleek fabric against her bare skin. She studied herself in the mirror. The color suited her well enough, but it would have looked even better on Caleb, she mused. The pajama's blue-green hue would darken the azure of his eyes, giving them hidden depths, while the soft, clinging silk would emphasize his well-muscled chest.

Lucy folded back the heavy quilt, turned out the lights, and climbed into bed, wiggling around in an attempt to find a comfortable spot. It wasn't easy. The bed was much firmer than her own well-worn mattress and the pillows much softer. Lucy punched them a few times before realizing that the problem was that they were down, and her own pillows a rather worn polyester. Finally, she piled both pillows together and bounced her head up and down on them a few times before closing her eyes in the hope of sleep. Five minutes later she was dead to the world.

It was the nagging pain in her stomach that woke her a couple of hours later. She rolled over onto her back and blinked at the white cloud over her head. She pushed a strand of hair out of her eyes, then smiled as she realized that the white blur was the underside of the canopy.

Her stomach growled protestingly, and Lucy sighed. She was starved. She'd been so nervous at dinner that she'd barely tasted the delicious food she'd prepared, and she'd skipped lunch at work. The piece of toast she'd consumed at breakfast seemed a long way away.

What time was it? Lucy frowned curiously at the windows, but their thick drapes effectively blocked the outside. Sitting up, she switched on the lamp on the bedside table and glanced at the small alarm clock. Four-fifteen. At least three hours until breakfast, and quite possibly four. It was Saturday, and Caleb probably slept late on the weekend. Her stomach gave another grumble, and she thought longingly of the refrigerator in which he had been rummaging around. What she wouldn't give for just a few minutes with its well-stocked interior!

Why not? Granted, it was hardly polite to help yourself to your host's food, but she doubted he'd mind. Or
even find out, for that matter. Presumably he was fast
asleep. There was no one else in the house for her to
disturb. All she had to do was to creep down the stairs,
make herself a quick snack, and sneak back. No one
would ever be the wiser.

Another loud rumble from her stomach decided her.
She'd never be able to get back to sleep until she placated
it. Lucy slipped out of bed, grimacing as she caught a
glimpse of herself in the dresser mirror. She looked like
an advertisement for a night of debauchery. Her long red
hair had come loose and now tumbled down her back.
Her pajama top was partially unbuttoned and had slipped
off one white shoulder, exposing a vast expanse of creamy
white skin, while the full length of her long legs showed
beneath the brief hem.

Hastily, Lucy adjusted the top, rebuttoning it and tugging at the bottom. What she really needed was a robe,
but Caleb hadn't offered her one. Perhaps he hadn't any,
she thought, remembering the casual way he had run
around in his abbreviated running shorts. Modesty didn't
seem to be one of his strong points.

For a brief moment Lucy considered wrapping herself
in the quilt from the bed, but she dismissed the idea as
Victorian. In the first place, she wasn't likely to meet
anyone. In the second, she wasn't really indecent. At
least, she wasn't if she remembered not to bend over.

Cautiously, Lucy opened her bedroom door and peeked
out into the hallway, which was dimly illuminated by a
light near the back stairwell. Satisfied that no one was
around, she crept down the hallway and scampered down
the stairs.

The outside floodlights provided plenty of light in the
kitchen as Lucy made a beeline for the refrigerator. It
opened quietly, and her eyes widened at the bounty it
revealed. She didn't want to start heating things in an

unfamiliar kitchen, so she decided to settle for a sandwich and a glass of milk.

She set the remains of a beef roast on the counter along with lettuce, tomatoes, Swiss cheese, mayonnaise, and a half-gallon of milk. She located bread, and was hungrily slicing thick pieces of the beef when a voice from directly behind her made her shriek and drop the knife on the floor.

Caleb leaned down and picked up the knife. "Be careful. You're liable to slice your toes off." He rinsed off the knife and handed it back to her.

He *did* have a bathrobe, Lucy acknowledged, noticing the short navy terrycloth robe he was wearing. His bare legs were visible below its knee-length hem, as was a great deal of bare chest. Lucy forced her mind away from the realization that Caleb slept in the nude.

"You startled me! What are you doing down here?"

"It is my kitchen," he said dryly. "I heard you sneaking past my door and wondered what you were up to."

"I was hungry," she muttered in embarrassment. Somehow raiding your host's food supply seemed worse when he caught you at it.

"I don't suppose you'd be willing to share?" he asked hopefully.

"Certainly." Lucy smiled, suddenly feeling light-hearted. "You pour the milk and I'll make the sandwiches. What do you want on yours?"

"Everything." He eyed the stack of food with approval.

The sandwiches were quickly made, and Lucy followed Caleb up the stairs with a heaped plate. He pushed open her bedroom door, almost spilling the milk he was carrying.

"Careful," Lucy automatically cautioned him and then bit her lips. It was hardly her place to correct him, but he didn't seem to mind.

"Climb into bed," he ordered. "We'll eat there."

Lucy set the plate of sandwiches down on the bedside

table and climbed in, thankfully shoving her long legs under the covers. His matter-of-fact air—as if they were two friends on a picnic—had almost made her forget that it was the middle of the night and that between them they weren't wearing a decent outfit.

Caleb merely smiled at her. He obviously saw her as a sexless friend. Stifling a sigh, Lucy smiled back, refusing to allow her unease to show. She took the glass of milk he handed her, picked up a hefty sandwich, and began to munch it in companionable silence.

"You make a good sandwich, Lucy," Caleb complimented her when they'd eaten the last crumbs.

"Thank you, kind sir." She put down her empty glass and yawned prodigiously.

"Poor Lucy." Caleb smiled gently at her. "All that remains is for me to kiss you good night and tuck you into bed."

Lucy shivered at the intimate sound of his words. Her tongue darted out to lick her suddenly dry lips. The lateness of the hour, the location of their picnic, and the tiredness of her mind were combining to create an atmosphere of intimacy. She blinked uncertainly when Caleb leaned over and gently pushed her back into the soft mound of down pillows. His face was a mask of total concentration as his fingertips began lightly tracing her features. They skimmed slowly over her eyebrows, traced under one of her widening eyes, over the bridge of her nose, and under the other eye, before continuing on to lightly outline her ear.

Lucy shivered slightly as his hand finished its exploration of her ear and slid down her throat, seemingly intent on exploring every inch of her. She stared up into his eyes, which seemed to glow from within. His face was totally absorbed. Like a blind man committing her features to heart, he continued his tactile exploration.

Lucy sucked in a lungful of air and closed her eyes on a sigh as his fingers left her throat and traced along her collarbone before gently stroking the soft swell of her breast visible in the deep neckline of the pajama top. A current of emotional electricity spread from the touch of his hand, and Lucy was unable to suppress a sigh of pleasure.

She forced open her heavy eyelids and glanced uncertainly into his face. What he was doing was obvious, even to her muddled mind. He was skillfully seducing her. He was carefully creating a fever pitch of sexual tension that begged for release. What wasn't so obvious was why. Why would Caleb Bannister want to make love to her? She opened her mouth to ask him, but all rational thought fled as she felt the damp warmth of his tongue as it lightly traced the hardening tip of her breast through the silk top.

"Caleb?" Lucy gasped uncertainly as she twisted slightly under his probing hands. He didn't bother to answer. Instead, his mouth began to map a leisurely path to her mouth. Lightly, he rubbed his lips over hers in a tantalizing, teasing gesture.

Eagerly, Lucy pulled his head down. His mouth hardened and deepened its pressure until she willingly opened her mouth to his invasion. His tongue flicked inside, stroking and exploring the velvety recesses.

Deep in her mind a warning bell rang. She should stop him now. She knew he'd quit if she asked him to. Caleb wasn't the kind of man to use force. He didn't have to. But Lucy allowed the sweet flood of feeling he was evoking to drown the voice of reason. Her hands slipped under his bathrobe. She ran her palms over his hair-roughened chest, taking satisfaction in the accelerated beat of his heart. He wasn't immune to her. Nor was he emotionally detached from what he was doing.

His mouth left hers and moved downward, dropping stinging little kisses as it went. Lucy felt a cool rush of air as his hands unbuttoned her top and pushed the material back, exposing her pale, gleaming flesh to his heated gaze.

"So lovely," his husky voice praised her. "So absolutely gorgeous." His large hands closed over her breasts, taking the full, soft weight of them in his palms. Idly, he flicked his thumbs over the dusky tips, growling with satisfaction as they hardened under his ministrations.

Lucy squirmed at the shards of sensation his fingers evoked and then gasped as his tongue began drawing circles around the hard pink tip of one swollen breast. Finally, his mouth closed over the throbbing flesh and began gently sucking.

"Caleb!" Lucy moaned. She threaded her fingers through the silky softness of his hair and held him against her breast. That he should stop now was unthinkable. Every nerve ending in her body was on fire.

Caleb increased the pressure his mouth was exerting almost to the point of pain. Lucy responded instinctively, arching her body against him. She wanted to feel the heaviness of him against her, but he held back. His mouth left her breasts and moved slowly downward, pausing for his tongue to teasingly outline her navel before darting inside in a devastating foray. Lucy gasped and twisted sideways, but his hands held her still as his tongue painted sensual patterns across the silken skin of her abdomen.

"Caleb! Caleb, please!" Lucy cried, her frantic body stoked to a blazing mass of need by his slow, unhurried exploration.

"Soon, darling, soon." His deep whisper promised ecstasy, but she barely heard him. She was too caught up in the maelstrom of her own feelings. Her whole being was centered on the warmth of his mouth and the feel of his hands. Nothing else existed.

His fingers followed his tongue, lightly stroking over her stomach before slipping between her legs to move them apart. He planted tantalizing kisses along the silky skin of her inner thighs as she gave soft cries of unfulfilled desire.

Finally, when Lucy thought she'd faint from the pressure building in her, Caleb eased off his robe, slipped between her legs, and lowered the full weight of his body along her heated flesh. The hair on his chest sanded the taut tips of her swollen breasts and she arched herself against him. She clutched the hard muscles of his broad shoulders and tried to pull him to her, but he wouldn't be hurried as he sensually rubbed his body over hers. Each tiny pinpoint of contact seemed to register its own frantic desire on her disoriented mind, demanding satisfaction—satisfaction Caleb seemed unwilling to grant.

"Caleb!" Lucy's voice was a hoarse sob as her hands clutched at him. Nothing on earth mattered but that he fill the aching void he'd created.

At last he moved, stilling her frantic thrashings with his own limbs. He let her feel the full, heavy weight of his body for a brief second before he completed the final embrace with a powerful thrust of his body.

Lucy gasped and her eyes widened at the incredible feeling which flooded her. Momentarily it was enough simply to be at one with him.

Caleb grasped her chin, holding her head still. Lucy stared up into his face, feeling no shyness, only a sense of rightness. His eyes had darkened to navy and there was a slight flush high on his cheekbones. His mouth was curled in a sensual smile, but Lucy was certain that he scarcely saw her. His whole being was concentrating on the feel of her willing body beneath his.

Gently he slipped his hands under her hips and held her tightly against him as he began to move in a rhythm as old as time itself.

Lucy closed her eyes, shutting out everything but the velvety pressure which was pushing her closer and closer to ecstasy. Her emotions seemed to be twisting tighter and tighter, until with a final movement, Caleb snapped the thread of sexual tension and sent her tumbling down into a golden world of incredible sensation. Dimly, her mind registered when Caleb took his own pleasure and collapsed breathlessly on her. Lucy ran gentle fingers over his damp flesh, reveling in the helpless feminine feeling the heavy crush of his body invoked.

He gathered her into his arms and rolled onto his back. His hands pressed her head against his chest.

"Sleep now, Lucy," he murmured. "Go to sleep," he repeated as his fingers smoothed the tangled hair from her flushed face.

She trustingly nuzzled her face into his damp chest and obediently closed her eyes, allowing the hypnotic movement of his caressing hand to send her into a deep, sated slumber.

CHAPTER
Seven

LUCY ROLLED OVER and stretched, then frowned slightly as her eyes focused on the cream-colored canopy.

Where was she? She tried to rally her tired mind. Caleb's guest room. The answer burst full-blown into her consciousness along with the recollection of what had happened here in the small hours of the morning. Lucy glanced frantically around the room, breathing a sigh of relief when she realized that she was alone. She needed time before she could face Caleb. Time to try to figure out what had happened. No, not *what* had happened, she thought wryly; that was obvious. What wasn't so obvious was *why*. Why would a sophisticated man of the world make love to her? More to the point, why would a sophisticated man of the world who preferred petite, green-eyed blondes make love to an oversized redhead?

Desperation? She dismissed the idea at once. Men who were desperate to take a woman to bed didn't use such infinite patience in seducing them. And it had been a seduction, Lucy remembered, a fantastically skillful manipulation of her senses. At no point had he applied force or coercion. She could have stopped him anytime she'd wanted to. The trouble was that she hadn't wanted to. Caleb made her conscious of her basic femininity in a way no man ever had and, Lucy had the disheartening feeling, ever would—so that when he'd finished up their impromptu picnic by making her the dessert, she'd not only raised no objections, she'd actively welcomed his attentions.

But where did Caleb's feelings fit into all this? Lucy frowned. Could he have thought that she expected him to make love to her, and hadn't wanted to disappoint her? The awful thought was almost too shattering to contemplate, but Lucy forced herself to face it. She had been wearing a little bit of silk that revealed more than it covered. But, on the other hand, he'd been the one who had given it to her. However, he'd merely left it in her room. Clearly he hadn't expected to see her wearing it. He'd have had no way of knowing that she'd take it into her head to go wandering about his house at four in the morning.

Then, too, there was the manner in which he'd made love to her. There'd been no hurried, impatient fumbling to slake an overwhelming desire on his part. His whole demeanor had been that of a man bent on satisfying a woman, of bringing her to full awareness of her own body and its potential for sexual pleasure.

But she'd pleased him, she argued mentally. She wasn't so naive as not to know that he'd found a great deal of pleasure in making love to her. But had the pleasure come from making love to her in particular, or would any available woman have sufficed?

Try as she might to rationalize it away, the conclusion was inescapable. Caleb had joined her for a snack, and something in her manner had led him to believe that she wanted him to make love to her. So he had. It was as simple as that. He liked her as a person and hadn't wanted to hurt her feelings by rebuffing her. He was experienced enough to find pleasure with her, despite the fact that she was so far from his usual tastes. What was that old saying? Lucy grimaced. All cats are gray in the dark.

So where did that leave her? She was going to have to face him—and soon, she thought, glancing at the clock on the bedside table. It was nine-thirty. She could hardly hide in the bedroom all day. He was bound to have plans for Saturday. Plans that didn't include her. And she needed to get back and wait for the air-conditioner repairman.

The thought of her apartment brought Beth to mind for the first time that morning and Lucy groaned in dismay. How could she have forgotten Beth! My God, she chastised herself, she'd blithely gone to bed with the man she was trying to help her best friend marry. However, although Beth might want to marry Caleb, there had as yet been no concrete evidence that he was similarly inclined. He'd been polite last night and solicitous of Beth's comfort, but then he'd done as much for the other female members of the party. What a mess, Lucy thought with a sigh. And she'd complicated the whole situation beyond belief by going to bed with him.

Her unhappy thoughts were interrupted when the door opened quietly and Caleb peeked in.

Lucy's eyes ran hungrily over his large frame, noting the breadth of his shoulders under his knit shirt and the long length of muscular leg exposed by his white tennis shorts. He seemed to be his usual cheerful self. It was as if last night had never occurred. A curious pain twisted through Lucy, but her pride came to her rescue. She had no intention of letting him see just how devastating she'd found the experience of sharing his bed. If he wanted to pretend amnesia about last night, so be it. He need have no fears that she was going to try to make any claims on him based on one night's lovemaking.

Lucy forced herself to meet his eyes. It was one of the hardest things she'd ever done. The knowledge of what had happened here in this room seemed to hang between them like a dark cloud, but Lucy was not one to indulge in either wishful thinking or self-recrimination. The problem wouldn't go away. It had to be faced, and faced in such a way that it didn't destroy the tenuous friendship they'd forged. That was essential to her. She had to make him believe that she attached no more importance to what had happened last night than he did.

"Good morning," Lucy managed to say through dry lips. "I'm sorry I slept so long. I hope I haven't kept you from anything." Or anyone, she thought silently, noting his wary reaction. It was all she needed to harden her resolve. He had obviously been worried she was going to cling and cause a scene. Lucy became all the more determined to play the role of the cool sophisticate who saw nothing untoward about waking up in a strange bed.

"You haven't." He came into the room. "I was out jogging. I considered waking you up, but you looked so peaceful sleeping that I didn't have the heart." His eyes gleamed with secret knowledge, and Lucy instinctively retreated further under the covers. He grinned as he watched her withdraw, and she bit back an urge to say something trite. She'd feel much more in command of the situation if she had some clothes on, but there was no way in the world she could calmly leave the protection of the sheets and dress under his interested gaze. That sophisticated she wasn't.

"I'm going to teach you some stretching exercises this morning before you try jogging again." He tossed some clothes on the bed. "I thought you'd rather borrow something of mine than go home in an evening dress."

"Thank you," Lucy agreed. It would look rather debauched coming in at noon from a date the night before. Not that she put a great deal of emphasis on what people thought, but there was enough of her small-town upbringing in her makeup for her to prefer not to flout the conventions. "But you can forget stretching exercises. I'm tall enough as it is."

"They don't stretch *you*, they stretch your muscles. It's essential that you get in the habit of warming up before you run, or you're liable to do something like pull a hamstring."

"I thought only men had hamstrings," she murmured, diverted.

"You need a few anatomy lessons." Caleb's eyes

gleamed with devilment. "I'll show you where your hamstring is. I've always felt that people remember better when they have firsthand experience. Or better still, since you seem to have a preference for masculine hamstrings, I'll let you feel mine." He grinned at her wolfishly.

His words drew Lucy's eyes to the taut line of his thighs, and her stomach contracted as she thought of running her fingers over his hard muscles.

"That's not necessary." She gulped, tearing her gaze away. "I'll take your word for where it is."

"Pity." He sighed. "But we can discuss it later. You get dressed and I'll show you the exercise before breakfast."

"I should go right home." She made a half-hearted attempt to free him from the obligation to entertain her. "The repairman might be there already."

"He's come and gone," Caleb told her. "I called your superintendent this morning before I went out to run, and he promised to let the man in at eight. Your apartment should be back to normal by the time you get there."

"Thank you." Lucy gave up trying to find excuses to leave and accepted his apparent willingness to feed her.

"Hurry up. I'm starved!"

As he closed the door behind him, Lucy expelled her breath. She'd done it. She'd managed to act as if nothing out of the ordinary had happened, and it appeared that he was going to buy it. It also appeared that they were back on their old footing of casual friendliness. She breathed a sigh of relief. It wasn't what she really wanted, but it was infinitely better than his calmly taking her home and severing their acquaintance.

Lucy picked up the navy jogging shorts on the bed and slipped into them, grateful they had an elastic waistband. They didn't really fit, but neither were they in danger of falling off.

She pulled on the white knit shirt and giggled at her reflection in the mirror. She looked ludicrous—not at all like the ultra-sophisticated types Caleb favored. The thought depressed her momentarily until she remembered that he apparently hadn't forgotten his vow to teach her to jog. While being thought of as a jogging partner hardly compared with being seen as a desirable, sexy woman, it was better than not being thought of at all.

She found him in the back room. He was sitting on the couch, his large feet propped up on the coffee table, reading the morning paper. The domestic scene gave Lucy a curious pang, which she promptly attributed to hunger. She must not start getting sentimental about Caleb Bannister. It was bad enough that she was sexually attracted to him.

"Ah, there you are." He smiled at her over the top of the newspaper, and Lucy's treacherous heart did a flip-flop. "Come on. I'll show you your exercise first, and then we'll eat." He tossed the paper to the floor.

"How about if we eat first?" she suggested. "Exercising on an empty stomach sounds vaguely obscene."

"You'll get cramps if you do it on a full stomach. Besides," he scoffed, "this isn't a real exercise. It's simply a pre-running stretch. Come over here."

Sighing, Lucy went. She doubted if anyone had ever talked Caleb Bannister out of anything he'd wanted to do. Certainly no woman had.

"Stand beside that chair." He nodded toward a cream-colored easy chair. "Put one leg up on the arm."

Lucy did, feeling like an absolute idiot.

"Now lean over and touch your toes."

Lucy leaned, but her toes were definitely out of reach. "Augh," she moaned. "This isn't a stretching exercise. It feels more like a ripping one."

"Try again," he encouraged her. "No one could be that out of shape."

Lucy muttered nastily as she reached for her elusive toes again. She gasped as she felt a large hand grasp the top of her thigh and slip up under the loose leg of the borrowed shorts.

"What are you doing?" She winced to hear herself.

She sounded like a frightened virgin instead of a self-possessed, liberated woman.

"I'm trying to show you what you're supposed to be stretching. Now pay attention to what I'm doing."

Pay attention! Lucy's mind reeled as his hand cupped the tense muscles of her hip. Every cell in her body was focused on the feel of that hand.

"The hamstring starts here in your hip." He gently kneaded the spot.

Lucy expelled her breath to the silent count of three, praying that he wouldn't realize just how affected she was by his casual touch. It would blow forever her image as a cool, self-confident friend.

"It continues down the back of your thigh..." Her muscles contracted even tighter as his hand massaged them, but she was unable to stop the instinctive reaction. "...down your calf, and ends at the ankle. When it pulls, it usually goes at the ankle."

"Oh?" Lucy greeted the information with a total lack of interest.

"Here." He took her hand and put it on her calf. "Feel how tight you are."

"Yup," Lucy agreed.

"Now, then. Put your leg down a second." Lucy did, glad of the respite. It seemed that last night, rather than satisfy her desire for Caleb, had merely enhanced it, making her all the more responsive to his every movement.

Caleb lifted his leg onto the chair arm, leaned over, and grabbed his whole foot in one hand.

"Show-off," Lucy muttered.

"Oh, I've got lots of hidden talent." His eyes gleamed wickedly. Lucy hurriedly looked away, unwilling to face the intimate knowledge in his teasing glance. "Now, feel my hamstring between my hip and knee."

"What?" Lucy's eyes were drawn to his powerfully muscled leg with its liberal covering of light blond hair.

"Touch it!" he ordered in exasperated tones. "I'm

trying to show you the difference a good exercise program can make in your muscles."

"Oh." Lucy gingerly prodded the muscles in question with a diffident forefinger.

"Not like that, for God's sake. Feel it!"

Lucy's fingers closed over his leg and squeezed. It really was a lot looser than hers, she acknowledged silently. Not that she cared. Having loose muscles was not very high up on her list of priorities. Why, she'd managed to exist twenty-seven years without even knowing that she possessed a hamstring.

Exist was right, a corner of her mind registered. She seemed to have merely been existing instead of living, until Caleb Bannister had appeared on the scene. And what would happen once he left? A feeling of desolation swept through her.

"There's no reason to look so forlorn at the difference, Lucy. A few weeks and you'll be as limber as I am."

Lucy blinked, then jumped back as she realized that she was still holding his leg.

"I doubt it." She let his misinterpretation of her thoughts stand. She could hardly tell him what she'd really been thinking about.

"Hurry up, woman." He straightened up. "Finish your exercise. I want my breakfast."

Lucy obliged, simply because it was easier to give in to him than it was to argue.

"You've almost got the hang of it," he allowed once she had finished. "Come on out to the kitchen and have a little something to eat."

"A little something" turned out to be a bag of onion bagels, still warm from the oven, a tub of cream cheese, lox, and a huge bowl of fresh strawberries.

"Here." He handed her a large glass filled to the brim with icy orange juice.

Lucy took a sip, although the size of the tumbler depressed her. It was further proof that Caleb saw her as one of the guys, complete with a man's appetite. He'd never have given a glass of juice that size to one of the model types he normally dated—to say nothing of offering them bagels and cream cheese. They probably didn't even eat breakfast.

"Don't you like bagels?" Caleb caught her expression. "I could make you an omelet."

Lucy forced a bright smile. "I love bagels." She split one and spread the cream cheese with a liberal hand. As long as he thought of her as a man, she might as well eat like one.

"Have some lox." He pushed the carton filled with pale pink slices at her.

"No, thanks." Lucy wrinkled her nose in distaste. "It smells like dead fish."

"Well, it is. Dead smoked salmon," he replied reasonably as he piled lox on his own bagel.

An hour later, Lucy, in bare feet and her borrowed outfit, was letting herself into her apartment. She'd felt ridiculous walking through the lobby wihout shoes, but wearing last night's dressy sandals would have proclaimed to all and sundry that this was the morning after the night before.

For once the superintendent had been telling the truth, and her apartment was blessedly cool. Lucy breathed a sigh of relief.

Fifteen minutes later, after she'd had a quick shower and changed into a pair of her own jeans and a faded green T-shirt, the doorbell rang.

Her heart jumped, and for one moment she allowed herself to hope that Caleb had returned. Common sense reasserted itself. He'd left her not half an hour ago without so much as a kiss. His "Take care" had been casual in the extreme, especially considering what had happened last night. It had chilled Lucy, forcing her into a matching coolness. She'd managed to sound casual to the point of indifference when he'd promised to call. Much as she wanted to believe he would, she was afraid to build up her hopes.

"Oh, Lucy!" Beth rushed into the room the second Lucy had taken off the chain.

"Hi," Lucy weakly greeted her friend, thoroughly ashamed of the fact that in her preoccupation with Caleb she'd forgotten to call Beth. God, what a mess, she thought as she closed the door behind her. "Come and have a cup of coffee. It ought to be done by now."

"I'm so glad you're up, Lucy!" Beth poured herself coffee. "I didn't want to disturb you so I waited, but I just couldn't wait any longer."

"It's okay. I've been up for quite a while." Lucy made a production of adding milk and sugar to her coffee. Apparently Beth didn't realize that Lucy had spent the night with Caleb—a fact Lucy was loath to impart, especially when it looked very much like he was trying to forget it, too. Besides, what could she say? Oh, by the way, remember that man I'm helping you to catch? Well, I slept with him last night, but it's all right because this morning he doesn't want to know. Hardly, Lucy thought sourly. Far better to try and wipe last night's fiasco from her mind and go on from there. Lucy took a sip of coffee and followed Beth back into the living room.

"I see your air conditioning got fixed," Beth commented. "I thought you might come by last night."

"I didn't need to. I was very comfortable," Lucy replied honestly, hoping Beth wouldn't ask any more questions. She needn't have worried. Beth was so full of her own plans that Lucy and her temperamental air conditioning rated no more than a passing thought.

"Oh, Lucy," Beth bubbled with enthusiasm, "wasn't he magnificent! He's so handsome and charming and those muscles . . ." Beth sighed. "I get goose bumps just looking at him."

"But what about the man behind the muscles and the

thousand-dollar suit?" Lucy asked dryly.

"What do you mean?" Beth sounded confused.

"I mean, my friend, that muscles are well and good, but you have to live with the man. Forget the trimmings. What about the man?"

"I don't know." For a moment Beth sounded uncertain, but she quickly rebounded. "It's simply because he's such a reserved person. It's hard to get a handle on what he's really like."

"Reserved!" Lucy stared at Beth. Caleb seemed to her to be about as reserved as an explosion. But that was probably because he considered her to be one of the guys, whereas he saw Beth as an attractive, eligible woman and treated her accordingly.

"You know what I mean, Lucy. He's polite, but he never says anything personal. Everything is very . . . very . . ." Beth broke off as if trying to find an adequate adjective. "Very formal," she finally finished weakly. "But I don't care about that. I didn't pick him out because of what kind of man he was. I picked him out because of what he *has,* although I'm willing to admit that his looks are a plus."

"Good for you." Lucy sighed.

"You aren't getting cold feet, are you?" Beth demanded.

"No."

"Was he nasty to you when he brought you home last night?" Beth asked curiously. "I wanted to wait and come back with you two."

"Then why didn't you?"

"Because I wasn't really given a choice," Beth replied dryly. "I don't know exactly what happened while I was dancing with Tom and you were in the ladies' room. But apparently, Linda finally pushed John too far, because when I got back to the table, he told her in no uncertain terms that they were leaving. It was horribly embarrassing. Everyone was staring. Then Caleb ordered the Glassons to take me home. Oh, it was all done in that polite manner of his, but somehow we all left exactly as instructed."

Briefly Lucy considered telling Beth why John had been so angry, but decided against it. It would serve no useful purpose, and Lucy wasn't proud of her own part in the affair.

"So tell me, what did he say?" Beth demanded.

"Nothing," Lucy replied honestly.

"Nothing?" Beth repeated, her disappointment evident in the drop of her soft mouth. "He should have said something."

"Should he have?" Lucy queried.

"Ask your computer if Caleb talks about his feminine interests."

"All right." Lucy obediently set down her coffee and went into the den, where she keyed the question into the terminal. A second later a bright green NO appeared on the screen.

"Ha!" Beth exclaimed. "There you are. It's a good sign that he didn't say anything about me."

"At least it's not a bad one," Lucy agreed.

"I've been thinking, Lucy." Beth chewed thoughtfully on her thumbnail. "Maybe I could call him tonight and invite him out. I could say someone gave me two tickets to the opera."

"That line's as old as the hills!" Lucy scoffed. "Besides, he might not like the opera."

"Ask the computer."

Lucy keyed in the question and watched as another NO lit the screen.

"Ask about the ballet."

Lucy did, and was again rewarded by a NO.

"Drat!" Beth complained. "He doesn't like anything I do."

"You aren't marrying him for his interests, you're marrying him for his money!" Lucy snapped and was immediately repentant when Beth's face fell. "Sorry about that." Lucy sighed. "Why don't we see what kind of things he does like?" The answer was not long in coming. Nor did Beth find it pleasing.

"Basketball, baseball, football, track," Beth read the printout in dismay. "The only things that even sound vaguely promising are the symphony and the arts—although it probably means he buys art as an investment."

"Probably," Lucy agreed, remembering some of the magnificent paintings in his home.

"So now what?" Beth queried.

"Nothing, for the moment," Lucy volunteered. "You've met the man. Give him a chance to respond. If you start chasing him, he'll run."

"Lucy, *you* could call him..." Beth began.

"Lucy did call, and Lucy has no intention of calling again. Caleb knows where we are. If he wants to get in touch, he will." Not even her friendship with Beth would induce her to call Caleb a second time. The next move had to be his. Her lacerated pride demanded it.

CHAPTER
Eight

LUCY PATTED THE complicated knot of hair on the back of her head as she studied her reflection in her bedroom mirror. The style suited her, giving her an air of sophisticated elegance—which was totally at variance with the uncertain confusion in the depths of her eyes. Nervously, she inspected her makeup for flaws, finding none. The eye shadow enhanced and enlarged her chocolate-brown eyes, adding mysterious depths, while the orange-rust gloss coating her soft lips gave them a moist gleam.

Lucy wasn't quite so certain about her dress. She glanced thoughtfully down at it. The gown was a romantic fantasy that she had fallen in love with the first time she'd seen it. It was like something out of a Victorian dream. Made of cream silk, it had a high neck, long full sleeves with deep cuffs, a close-fitted tucked bodice, and a floor-length skirt that ended in a deep flounce. The whole affair was lavishly trimmed with hand-crocheted ivory lace. It was a beautiful dress, but it was also the type of outfit Lucy usually avoided, feeling that lace and ruffles were more suited to someone of Beth's petite size. But somehow she hadn't been able to pass this one up. She had bought it specifically for this evening, even though she knew that Caleb Bannister preferred high-fashion garments to romantic gestures from the past.

At any rate, it wasn't going to matter, she told herself. Caleb was hardly likely to bother with her when Beth was along.

Lucy frowned slightly as she remembered the phone call that had set up this evening. After she'd left him last Saturday morning she had waited, hoping that he'd call, but the phone had remained discouragingly silent until the following Wednesday. He'd called in the early evening—from Switzerland, of all places—and had asked her and Beth out for Saturday night. It seemed he was entertaining an out-of-town client and wanted them to make up a foursome. Lucy had fallen all over herself to accept, although she'd lacked the courage to ask whose date she was supposed to be. For one thing, she feared he'd think she was trying to make demands on him and, for another, she was afraid of the answer. As long as he didn't actually tell her that she was merely along to placate some business acquaintance, she could continue to indulge in the fantasy that he found her fascinating.

The doorbell interrupted her musings and, giving her hair a final pat, she went to let in Beth.

"How do I look?" Beth twirled through the door in a swirl of black silk. She pirouetted and dropped Lucy a deep curtsy.

"My God!" Lucy blinked as she studied the dress. If Caleb really was partial to high fashion, then he'd love Beth's gown. A full silk skirt was attached to the shirt-waist top of black chiffon, on which brilliant red roses had been hand-painted. The dress was meant to be worn with nothing under it, so that the wearer's every movement afforded tantalizing glimpses of bare breasts. It was not a style that many would have either the panache or the figure to carry off, but fairness made Lucy admit that Beth's small, high breasts fit the style to perfection.

Lucy felt a momentary irrational envy, which she quickly squelched. If this was what Caleb really wanted in a woman, then there was no way that Lucy herself was ever going to be able to compete.

"I bought it through a friend who models," Beth told her. "She can get things she's shown at a terrific discount. Otherwise, I'd never have been able to afford it. According to your computer, this should be exactly the kind of thing he likes."

"I would imagine any normal, red-blooded male would like it," Lucy said tartly.

"Don't be stuffy," Beth said with a giggle. "Bare bosoms are all the fashion. Besides, I'm not exactly bare. It's only when the flowers shift that you can kind of get teasing glimpses."

"Then pray they don't wilt!"

"Oh, Lucy, I'm so excited!" Beth ran her fingers through her artfully disarranged blond curls. "It was a good thing we waited, just like your program said to. Thank God, Caleb called you to set up the date and not me. I can't seem to find anything to say to the man, and long silences on the phone are deadly."

"He's not so hard to talk to," Lucy protested.

"He is to me!" Beth grimaced. "All he has to do is fix those steely-blue eyes on me and my mind goes blank."

"And you want to marry him?" Lucy lifted a russet eyebrow.

"I don't intend to do much talking after we're married," Beth quipped, and Lucy was appalled at the strength of the jealousy that shook her. Despite the knowledge that she had no right to be jealous, she still was.

"Tell me again about this guy he's bringing along for you." Beth unwittingly echoed Lucy's own conclusions about who was escorting whom.

"All I know is that he's a client."

"Perhaps—" Beth began, only to be interrupted by the doorbell. Lucy waited a moment for Beth to position herself on the sofa before she opened the door.

An intense wave of pleasure at just seeing Caleb washed over her, and she desperately fought to keep her expression casual.

"Hi," she greeted him, glancing approvingly at the expertly tailored black evening jacket. The pristine whiteness of his tucked shirt set off the bronze tan of his skin.

Caleb didn't reply. He simply ran a gentle fingertip

over her cheek by way of a greeting. Lucy's eyes widened and her stomach twisted in response to his casual caress. He moved into the apartment and Lucy turned in relief to the man who'd been almost hidden behind Caleb's massive frame.

Her spirits sank as she studied the stranger. His curly brown hair, merry brown eyes, and friendly smile barely registered. What most impressed her was that he was at least four inches shorter than she. Suddenly, she felt overdressed and oversized, like an adult who'd inadvertently wandered into a children's party.

"Lucy, this is Joel James. Joel, Lucy Travers."

"Hello." Lucy allowed none of her feelings to show. The evening was going to be awkward enough without everyone guessing how much she hated towering over her date. She considered exchanging her heels for a pair of flats, but dismissed the idea. It would be too obvious. Besides, she didn't really have any flats that would do justice to her dress.

"Good evening, ma'am." Joel smiled charmingly at her, and Lucy could have kissed him. At least she'd been spared some idiot crack about Amazons.

She moved aside to follow the men into the living room and then almost tripped over Joel as he stopped dead, staring at Beth as if he'd never seen a woman before.

Lucy glanced curiously at Caleb to see his reaction to the truly gorgeous picture Beth made. But he was looking at her, his eyes gleaming with laughter as he invited her to share his silent mirth over Joel's bemusement. Apparently Caleb was so certain of his ability to attract Beth that Joel's blatant admiration didn't worry him at all. Lucy stiffened, then moved to perform the necessary introductions.

She left Joel seated beside Beth on the couch and went into the kitchen, not realizing that Caleb was right behind her until she turned and almost fell into his arms.

"I swear I'm going to buy you a bell to warn me where

you are—you're worse than a cat!" she snapped.

"But Lucy"—he laughed—"you don't have to wonder where I'm at. Just look behind you and I'll be there."

"You're more likely to be ahead of me!" she said tartly. "What do you want?"

"Two things." He smiled as he moved forward a step, bringing him into contact with her soft curves.

"First this." He gently cupped her face in his large hands, and leaning forward, lightly brushed her lips with his.

Lucy's eyes slid shut and she tilted her head back to better accommodate the caress. There was no thought of backing away. She'd been starving for the feel and taste of him since last Saturday, and she intended to indulge herself.

At her small sign of acceptance, Caleb's arms encircled her, drawing her closer to him. His hands slipped under her rounded buttocks, lifting her into him—an action that left her in no doubt about his reaction to her.

"Caleb." Lucy sighed as he feathered a light row of kisses down her neck, pausing to flick his tongue over the tiny pulse that fluttered in her throat. She squirmed against him, maddened by the insubstantiality of his kisses, but too uncertain of him to risk making any demands. Fortunately, he seemed to have no trouble interpreting her needs. With a husky chuckle he captured her chin with hard fingers and covered her lips with his. This time there was nothing tentative or teasing about the contact. His hunger seemed to match her own, and he was not averse to letting her see it.

Lucy's mouth opened under the pressure of his, and his tongue slipped inside to explore the silken recesses. She moaned deep in her throat as his hand covered her breast and his fingers gently tugged on the sensitive tip through the thin cloth of her dress. Tiny shards of sensation spread from the contact, invading her limbs and leaving her boneless. Lucy leaned into him, letting his body support her pliant form as she concentrated on the feel of his exploring tongue and the dizzying movements of his fingers. Her breast hardened, its tip standing taut against his chest while her stomach contracted with an ache that begged fulfillment.

Much too soon, Caleb put his hands on Lucy's shoulders and held her back from his body. He rested his forehead on hers and looked deep into her passion-filled eyes.

"Much as I'd like to continue this, I think we'd best quit now before I wind up making love to you on the kitchen floor."

"Why not?" Lucy muttered, not surfacing from the sensual fog that enshrouded her mind.

"Don't tempt me, love." He dropped a quick, hard kiss on her swollen lips. "The way I feel right now, I'd attempt it with you in a snowbank, but we have guests in the next room who are liable to come looking for their drinks. I wouldn't want them to get the wrong idea about you."

His words were like a dash of cold water across her heightened senses. Obviously he didn't want Beth to know that he was romancing Lucy in the kitchen. So why had he kissed her? She'd have been willing to swear that he'd been as involved in their lovemaking as she'd been herself. Unless . . . Her skin crawled at the thought. Could he really want Beth, but simply be using Lucy as a substitute? The idea was too painful to contemplate. She forced her jerky limbs to move away from the circle of Caleb's arms.

"You said two things." Her voice was high and uneven. She paused to steady it and continued doggedly, hoping her dismay wasn't visible.

"Lucy?" Caleb frowned and reached for her, but Lucy moved out of reach.

"You've got lipstick all over your mouth," she said tonelessly, "and we wouldn't want anyone to see it."

Caleb glanced sharply at her, but obediently took the paper towel she held out and scrubbed off the color.

"Actually, Lucy, I was hoping for scavenger rights to your refrigerator. I missed lunch, and I'm starving."

"Help yourself." She gestured toward the refrigerator. "I'll get the drinks ready."

Caleb rummaged inside before emerging with a chicken drumstick, a good-sized hunk of Monterey jack cheese, and a pleased expression. He perched on the tiny kitchen table and devoured his snack while Lucy placed the drinks on a tray.

She kept up a cheerful flow of chatter, more to discourage him from saying anything she didn't want to hear than for any other reason.

They returned to the living room to find Beth and Joel deep in conversation on the couch. At least, Beth was talking and Joel was listening to her with the rapt concentration of a lovesick adolescent.

Lucy risked a quick peek at Caleb to see what he thought of Joel's obvious enthrallment, but no reaction was visible on his features.

"Oh, Lucy"—Beth took the glass of white wine Lucy handed her—"guess what? Joel is a rancher out west—with cows and everything!"

Lucy blinked, uncertain of what kind of response was called for, but Beth didn't wait for one. She bubbled on, rhapsodizing about the great outdoors while Joel sat watching her, mesmerized. His unabashed admiration seemed to be exactly what Beth needed to restore her usual animation, and she seemed well on her way to becoming her effervescent self.

Half an hour later, Caleb set down his empty whiskey glass and reminded them that they'd best be moving if they didn't want to miss the opening curtain. It was the first time Lucy had heard that they were going to the theater, and she wasn't sure whether she was glad or not. While normally she loved the theater, she wasn't certain she could keep her mind on the stage with Caleb seated beside her. He was showing an unfortunate tendency to dominate her thoughts to the exclusion of all else.

Joel was so totally absorbed with Beth that he seemed to forget he was supposed to be Lucy's date. He ignored Lucy as he tenderly helped Beth drape her scarlet shawl around her slim shoulders and then escorted her out the door.

Lucy avoided looking at Caleb as he took her arm in his firm grasp and steered her after the other couple. His manners were much too good for him to say anything to Joel about his walking off with the wrong woman, but Lucy was certain which of them Caleb preferred. She almost wished he'd said something to Joel. Much as her pride rebelled at being second best, she'd much rather be second best to a man she didn't care about than to Caleb.

The play they attended was a sparkling comedy that starred the woman Caleb had been dining with on the night Lucy had first seen him. Current gossip claimed that she was his present mistress. Lucy wondered if the actress was responsible for the excellent seats they were enjoying. She shot an oblique glance at Beth, only to see similar speculation on her face. Lucy spent the first act wondering whether Caleb planned on introducing them to the actress after the play, and then decided during the second act that he wouldn't, despite Joel's unbashed enthusiasm for the leading lady. Caleb would hardly want Beth to meet an old flame of his.

Her assumption proved correct. Once the play was ended, Caleb showed no inclination to linger. He gathered them up and shepherded them out of the packed theater.

Lucy watched Beth stare around her at the extravagantly dressed women and their elegant escorts. If Beth didn't quit gawking like a stage-struck teenager, Caleb was going to see through her sophisticated veneer. Lucy caught Beth's eye and frowned warningly, and Beth once again slipped into her role of sophisticate.

The club Caleb took them to for a late supper was a small, exclusive establishment full of secluded alcoves.

Lucy noted the heavy damask tablecloths and cut-glass vases filled with exquisite pink rosebuds at each table. She breathed a sigh of relief as she followed along behind the welcoming maître d'. The quiet, relaxed atmosphere was much more to her taste than the noisy, crowded nightclub they'd visited last week, although there was dancing here, too. A three-piece ensemble was providing gentle background music for the half-dozen or so couples swaying gently on the tiny dance floor.

Her spirits lifted at the possibility of dancing with Caleb, and she was further cheered by the promise of a good meal. She was starved! Lucy had neglected to ask him ahead of time exactly what his plans were. If she'd known that they weren't going to eat until this late, she'd have joined Caleb in his raid on the refrigerator.

She slipped into the chair he was holding for her and picked up the oversized, gold-embossed, red leather menu. She glanced down its length, amused to see the total absence of anything so crass as prices.

"A margarita?" Caleb had caught her amusement and smiled back at her.

"Yes, thank you." Lucy was inordinately pleased that he remembered what she'd had to drink last week, and she happily perused the menu. She chose the tournedos Rossini, despite Beth's lack of interest in anything more substantial than a salad. Lucy consoled herself that she wasn't the one trying to impress Caleb with a svelte figure. To her relief, the men ordered hearty meals.

As soon as the waiter had departed, Joel turned to Beth and asked her to dance—an offer Beth seemed pleased to accept. She eagerly took Joel's proffered hand and walked toward the dance floor.

Lucy watched them go, thinking how well matched they were. Beth's petiteness seemed exactly right next to Joel's wiry frame. The five-inch difference in their heights provided a nice contrast, as opposed to the almost ludicrous disparity of the fifteen inches between Beth and Caleb. But then, Beth's smallness was one of the things that appealed to Caleb. Lucy sighed and sipped her water.

"Lamenting Joel's interest in your friend?" Caleb asked, watching Lucy study the couple.

"Good God, no!" Lucy exclaimed. "It's impossible to get romantic about someone four inches shorter than you are. I'd have to go through life slouched over—and in flats, too."

"A terrible fate." Caleb picked up her hand.

Lucy shivered slightly at the sensation that feathered along her skin as he began to outline her slender fingers. In Caleb's huge hands her own seemed almost small.

He turned her hand over and carried it to his lips, where he placed a kiss on her palm.

Lucy smiled uncertainly and then gasped as his tongue flicked out and began tracing sensual patterns on her sensitive skin. Her stomach tightened and she moved restlessly, torn between enjoying the feeling his tongue was creating and horror at the conviction that he was simply amusing himself until Beth returned. But could he really be so fickle?

The waiter bringing the drinks provided her with an excuse to remove her hand from his without appearing obvious about it. She sipped her potent drink and leaned back in her chair, deciding to do some probing of her own.

"Joel seems quite smitten with Beth," she began. She wanted to know if Caleb was as impervious to Joel's rapt veneration, and Beth's encouragement of it, as he seemed to be.

"It comes from spending most of his time on a ranch, surrounded by a bunch of cows," Caleb said.

"I refuse to believe that there are no women in Wyoming."

"Not women like Beth." Caleb watched her dancing. "Beth is unique even in New York City. Can you doubt that she'd appear to be an angel straight out of a Botticelli painting to someone who spends most of his time in rough places?"

"No," Lucy agreed, appalled at the strength of her dismay at hearing Caleb describe Beth in such glowing terms. Such enthusiasm from an acknowledged connoisseur of women could only mean that Beth had succeeded in capturing his interest.

Somehow the implication that her program was working all too well was sufficient to utterly destroy her appetite. Lucy picked at her delicious meal. She felt entirely disgusted by her reaction, but she couldn't seem to help herself. She noticed Caleb giving her several sharp glances as she meticulously rearranged the food on her plate, but fortunately, he didn't comment on her ordering a meal which she then proceeded to ignore. And at those prices, too! She wouldn't have blamed him if he'd been annoyed.

They were drinking their after-dinner coffee when Beth began to quiz Joel about the wide-open spaces of Wyoming. Lucy listened idly, content to let Beth sparkle. Joel's admiration was exactly what the impetuous Beth needed to overcome her reticence in Caleb's presence. Her effervescence was affecting Caleb, too, Lucy thought drearily as she watched him smile indulgently into Beth's animated features.

"You can't begin to appreciate the beauty of Wyoming unless you actually see it," Joel insisted. "It's nothing like this"—he waved his hand comprehensively—"this artificial jungle you call New York City."

"I happen to like this artificial jungle," Lucy replied. "For which you ought to be grateful. If everyone were so enamored of your prairie, it would very quickly look like New York City."

"Lucy!" Beth reproached her, and then turned back to Joel, her eyes gleaming with the fervor of the newly converted. "I wish I could see Wyoming. It sounds so . . . so . . ."

"Empty?" Lucy supplied.

"Why don't you?" Joel said excitedly. "Why don't you come back with me on Wednesday? Caleb and I are going out to look over my land. I'm trying to convince him to find me financing to drill some natural gas wells. He plans on staying through the weekend. You could see quite a bit in that time. You could come too, Lucy," he added as an obvious afterthought.

"Oh, Lucy, isn't that a wonderful idea?" Beth exclaimed.

Lucy stole a quick glance at Caleb, disheartened to see a frown on his face. Was he displeased at Joel's invitation in general, or simply at her inclusion? She didn't know, but one thing was certain, neither man wanted her along. She had too much pride to force herself on them.

"I don't think—" Lucy began, but Caleb interrupted her.

"Why don't you come along, Lucy? Beth's certainly dying to go, and she can hardly come with us by herself."

This unexpected streak of conventionality in Caleb told Lucy all she needed to know about his intentions about Beth. He would hardly go through the trouble of dragging Lucy along unless he was determined to protect Beth's reputation. And good old Lucy gets assigned the role of chaperone, Lucy thought bitterly. She wanted to refuse, but the pleading in Beth's eyes, coupled with her own very real desire to spend time with Caleb under any circumstances, undermined her resolve, and she found herself agreeing.

"If I can get the time off on such short notice," she qualified, more for her pride's sake than because she feared she couldn't be spared. She knew her boss would let her go.

As if Lucy's capitulation signaled the end of the evening, Joel set down his empty cup and glanced at his watch.

"I had no idea it was so late," he said in surprise. "I'll see you home, Beth. You, too." He smiled vaguely at

Lucy, who wondered if he'd forgotten her name already.

Lucy glanced at Caleb, remembering how adriotly he'd managed to take her home alone last weekend, but tonight he made no attempt to separate her from Beth and Joel. And she realized he had made no attempt to dance with her this evening, either. Apparently he'd lost whatever interest he'd ever had in her. What was the saying? She searched her memory. Familiarity breeds contempt. Well, they'd gotten about as familiar as two people could, and it seemed to have bred indifference.

Lucy had no choice but to agree to Joel's offer. She didn't have the self-confidence to ask Caleb to run her back to her apartment. Besides, she and Beth were going to the same place. No doubt Caleb figured Beth would be safe from Joel if Lucy was along.

Joel left the two women in the lobby of their apartment building with an absent nod at Lucy and a soulful look at Beth that reminded Lucy of a cocker spaniel. They watched him leave and then entered the elevator.

"He seems to have fallen very hard on rather short acquaintance, hasn't he?" Lucy observed.

"Uh-huh." Beth giggled. "Small, green-eyed blondes seem to be a universal male fantasy."

"That dress—or lack of it—doesn't hurt either," Lucy said dryly. "Am I to take it that you aren't similarly attracted?"

"Oh, he's all right for an evening"—Beth shrugged her slim shoulders—"but Caleb's what I want for good. Can you really see me spending my life on a ranch in the middle of nowhere?"

"No," Lucy replied honestly, "but if you feel that way, why are you encouraging him? Believe me, flying out to Wyoming with him is some encouragement."

"Him *and* Caleb," Beth corrected her. "Use your head, Lucy. Joel will do perfectly to make Caleb jealous. If he thinks I'm getting interested in another man, he'll show his hand."

"I guess." The thought gave Lucy no comfort.

"Lucy, you won't back out, will you?" Beth pleaded. "This weekend in Wyoming is exactly what I need to work on Caleb. It's almost impossible to get him alone here. Why, even tonight Joel thought I was *his* date. I had to spend my time with him since Caleb wouldn't want to be rude to a client."

"No, I guess he wouldn't," Lucy agreed tiredly, although privately she wondered about that. Caleb was as capable of being rude as anyone.

CHAPTER
Nine

LUCY FROWNED AT the neatly folded piles of clothes in her beige suitcase. They should be adequate, she finally decided. From Joel's description, the resort where they would be staying sounded very similar to one in Arizona where she'd attended a data-base workshop last year. She expected it to be a large, lavish business center with all the amenities of a first-class hotel. It actually sounded like fun, and she would have been looking forward to her first trip to Wyoming except for the knowledge that she'd only been included to protect Beth's reputation.

Stop feeling sorry for yourself! She slammed the suit-case shut and locked it. No one was forcing her to go. If she hadn't the strength to avoid Caleb even when she knew that he only saw her as a friend, then she had no one to blame but herself. It wasn't as if he fed her a line or anything like that.

Her own advice only made her feel worse. She'd been such an easy touch that he hadn't even had to promise her anything before she'd fallen into his arms and his bed. The thought rankled.

Lucy picked up her suitcase and carried it into the living room, where she set it down by the door. She glanced at the clock and decided to give Beth five more minutes before she went to find her.

She studied her image in the mirror, checking to make sure her makeup was fresh and her hair in order. Work had been a mad scramble that morning. She'd intended to leave at noon, thereby giving herself plenty of time to finish packing and make their three o'clock flight out of Kennedy Airport, but as luck would have it the payroll system had gone awry again. Lucy had worked frantically until shortly after one o'clock trying to patch it together. She'd had a hectic dash home, and she still felt as if she were on a roller coaster.

At least she didn't look it, Lucy encouraged herself with a pleased glance at her outfit. She wanted to reinforce her image as a successful professional. The cream-colored linen pants hugged her long legs and fit snugly across her neatly rounded bottom. A paisley-print silk blouse in shades of brown and gold emphasized her fair coloring. A matching cream blazer had been tossed over her suitcase. Their final destination was in the foothills of the Rockies, and Lucy knew that it got quite cool in the mountains once the sun went down, even in August.

The doorbell chimed, and Lucy hurried to open it, eager to be on her way.

"Ready, Beth?" Lucy swung open the door and blinked in surprise when she saw Caleb. He wasn't supposed to be here! He and Joel were to have flown out to Wyoming this morning, leaving Beth and Lucy to follow on a later flight.

Lucy peered behind him, but there was no Beth. She ran her eyes over his tall frame, approving of the beige pants that molded his powerful length of leg, the yellow oxford cloth shirt, which was open at the neck, and his well-worn Harris tweed jacket.

"Wake up, woman, we're in a hurry." He dropped a swift kiss on her parted lips.

Lucy's eyes widened at the heady sensation that enveloped her at the pressure of his lips.

"Well, perhaps not that much of a hurry," Caleb amended as he reached for her, drawing her close to the scratchy tweed of his jacket. His mouth covered hers with a lesiurely thoroughness that suspended all rational thought. Finally, he set her back and dropped a gentle kiss on the tip of her nose.

Lucy gazed into his eyes as if mesmerized, watching the tiny lights flickering in their depths. This was awful, her appalled mind shrieked. His kisses now seemed to be affecting her more, not less. It was as if his caresses were addictive, leaving her more vulnerable with every additional exposure. It was also embarrassing. Caleb was too experienced a man not to recognize the completeness of her response. If she didn't get a grip on her emotions, he was bound to wonder at the mindless fervor with which she returned his casual kisses.

"Has the trip been called off?" Lucy followed him into the apartment, trying to hide the disappointment she felt at the thought. She hadn't realized until that moment just how much she'd been looking forward to spending a long weekend in his company.

"No." He handed her her purse and blazer and picked up her suitcase. "I had an unexpected meeting at the last minute, and I wasn't able to get away in time to make the flight this morning. So Joel took Beth with him, and I'm using her seat this afternoon. Joel tried to get hold of you this morning at work to tell you, but no one could find you."

"I was over at the computer site," Lucy answered, secretly reveling in this latest development. A trip west in Caleb's company—without Beth to divert his attention! She wondered, though, what he thought about letting Joel escort Beth, especially since Joel was so obviously taken with Beth. She wished Caleb were as smitten with her. Well, few things in this world ever worked out exactly the way you wanted them to. The trick was to take advantage of the breaks, and not dwell on what you couldn't have.

"Lucy! Are you all right?" He frowned at her. "You seem very abstracted. At least you do until I kiss you, but I can hardly keep kissing you."

"Why not?" She gave him a come-hither look she'd gleaned from an old Bette Davis movie.

"It would be bound to attract a lot of attention as we crossed town."

"I wouldn't bet on it," Lucy said dryly. "Two weeks ago I saw a man in a full Dracula costume, complete with long, bloody fangs, walking down the street. Do you know that I was the only person who stopped and turned around to stare? I swear that if I were to stand in the middle of Fifth Avenue and strip naked, no one would notice."

"Oh, I don't know about that." Caleb's eyes darkened as his gaze slowly skimmed the length of her body, seeming to touch her. "You don't even have to take your clothes off to get my attention. I've got a very good memory." His hand encircled one of her breasts, his finger drawing ever-tightening circles until it reached the peak, which hardened under the thin silk of her blouse.

"That wasn't exactly what I meant." Lucy's voice was uneven.

"No?" Caleb chuckled, then sighed. "Unfortunately, we haven't time to explore what you did mean. I've a taxi waiting downstairs. It's a long ride to JFK, and the traffic this time of day is brutal. Come along." He picked up her suitcase, took her arm, and hurried her out of the apartment.

As Caleb had predicted, the taxi ride across the city seemed endless, and they found themselves at the airport with very little time to spare. They hurriedly checked their bags, received their boarding passes, and arrived at the check-in point just as boarding began.

Lucy almost laughed as the bored-looking stewardess looked up in the middle of her welcome-aboard spiel and caught sight of Caleb. Her beautiful black eyes widened and a faint flush stained her lightly tanned skin. She gave Caleb her most seductive smile, but he merely smiled absently at the woman as he guided Lucy into the plane.

Lucy felt a momentary twinge of pity for the stewardess as she quickly patted her perfectly coiffed black hair. She wished she could simply tell her that she was wasting her time. Caleb was no more interested in black-haired beauties than he was in overly tall redheads.

Their seats were in first class—a new experience for Lucy. Her company subscribed to the theory that the back of the plane arrived at the same time as the front, so there was no need to pay extra for first class. She glanced around curiously.

Caleb noticed her interest. "I always travel first class. It's roomier, and at six-five I need all the room I can get."

"True," Lucy agreed, never having considered that point before.

"We have the two far seats," he said, consulting the tickets. "Do you want the window seat?"

"No!" Lucy stood back to let him enter first. "It's bad enough to have to feel what's happening without having to watch it, too."

"Are you afraid of flying?" He looked at her in amazement.

"Petrified!" Lucy sank into the gold plush seat. "And don't tell me that flying's safer than riding in a car. I'm perfectly aware of that, and it doesn't impress me in the least. Every time one of these things hits the ground with a shriek and a shudder, I'm sure it's the end."

"Tell you what, I'll distract you." Caleb's eyes gleamed with a mischievous light that Lucy distrusted.

"Thank you. I think," she muttered.

Lucy turned at the sound of yowls coming down the aisle. A plump woman of about fifty plunked down into the seat next to Lucy and set an animal carrying cage on the floor. The beast inside sounded like a furious wildcat, and Lucy surreptitiously edged closer to Caleb.

"Poor Fou-Fou," the woman crooned. "Does the nasty old cage make Mumsy's darlin' upset?"

Lucy bit her lip and shot a quick glance at Caleb, almost breaking into laughter at the incredulous expression on his face.

"He's so sensitive," the woman confided to Lucy.

"He certainly is beautiful," Lucy answered truthfully, as she eyed Fou-Fou's luxuriant long white hair. Fou-Fou was momentarily calm, and encouraged by the cat's purr, Lucy leaned over and pushed a finger through the bars to stroke him. Fou-Fou, however, took violent exception to such familiarity, and with a warlike hiss he scratched a furrow down Lucy's finger.

"You're upsetting Fou-Fou," the woman objected, frowning at Lucy.

"Fou-Fou's not the only one upset!" Lucy snapped, her anger equally divided between the beast, the woman, herself for being so stupid as to try to pet the animal in the first place, and Caleb, who seemed to derive much enjoyment from the situation. She could feel his large frame shaking with suppressed laughter. Really! The man had no compassion! Lucy glared at him.

"Poor Lucy." He grinned at her. "Let me see how much you upset poor Fou-Fou." He picked up her hand and studied the angry red scratch, catching her off guard when he raised her finger to his mouth and ran his warm tongue over her wound.

Lucy gasped as a hot flood of feeling spread from the moist warmth of his caressing tongue. She shifted slightly in reaction to the erotic sensation that tightened her stomach and spread lower.

Caleb watched her face from behind half-closed lids and, seemingly content with the reaction he observed, planted a final kiss on her finger before returning her hand to her lap.

Fortunately for Lucy's peace of mind, the flight attendant told them to buckle their seat belts, giving her a chance to regain her composure. Lucy watched the pudgy woman stow Fou-Fou under her seat, glad that at least one menace had been removed.

The pilot's welcoming speech barely registered on Lucy's consciousness. Nor did the steward's explanation of the use of oxygen masks and emergency exits. Lucy kept her eyes firmly focused on the tip of the magazine sticking out of the pocket of the seat in front of her while she waited in dumb resignation for what was to come.

No matter how often she'd tried to make herself believe that her fear of flying was irrational, she'd never been able to convince her subconscious. The minute the plane began to taxi down the runway, her mind began picturing fiery crashes. She'd tried everything from tranquilizers to deep breathing, but the tranquilizers had made her feel drunk and had taken the better part of a day to sleep off, while the deep breathing had caused her to hyperventilate and pass out. Finally she had given up, and now viewed flying as a torture to be endured.

The plane began picking up speed. Lucy gulped, closed her eyes, and tried reciting prayers, but the only one she could think of began, "Now I lay me down to sleep." Doggedly, she kept going, hoping that God would credit the thought if not the words.

Slowly at first, and then more swiftly, another emotion began to nibble at the edges of her fear-shrouded mind. Caleb's right hand was holding her clenched fist in his while his left was rhythmically rubbing the nape of her neck.

Lucy opened her eyes as the sensations from his caressing hand began to swamp her fear. Dimly she was aware that the plane was still picking up speed, but at the moment the most important fact was that Caleb's fingers were erotically caressing the tender skin behind her ears. She arched her neck against his gentle touch. The sickening lurch the plane made as it left the ground and became airborne was hardly worthy of notice.

"Better?" His voice was tender as he removed his hand, totally ignoring Fou-Fou's owner's scandalized sniff.

"Yes. Once we're in the air, I'm fine." Lucy smiled

gratefully at him. "I'm sorry to be so much trouble."

"Not at all." He dropped her hand into her lap and she felt bereft at the loss of physical contact. "Most people have an irrational fear or two. What you need now is a drink." He ordered two Bloody Marys from the stewardess, gave Lucy hers, and set his own on the tray in front of him.

"Drink that. Then try to get some sleep," he ordered. "It'll be two hours earlier when we get to Wyoming, so a nap should help you last until bedtime."

"And keep me from bothering you," Lucy added as he extracted a thick sheaf of papers from his brown leather briefcase and began to study them.

Lucy idly sipped her drink and tried not to feel hurt. After all, it was hardly Caleb's role to keep her amused during the flight. Obviously he would have work to do. A man as busy as he would hardly waste a cross-country flight making small talk with his traveling companion— especially when that traveling companion hadn't been of his own choosing.

Lucy took another gulp of her drink, then frowned as her glance lit on Caleb's glass. He'd ordered a Bloody Mary, she realized, and he shouldn't have. According to her program, he never drank anything but straight whiskey. He didn't even dilute it with ice or soda. Lucy frowned, trying to remember. Every time he'd had a drink when she'd been with him, it'd been whiskey. So what was he doing with a Bloody Mary? It was hardly an event to get agitated about, but somehow it gave her a curiously vulnerable feeling whenever he reacted differently from the computer's predictions.

Forget it, she thought, draining the rest of her drink and beginning to munch on the ice cubes. She of all people should know the fallibility of her program.

Lucy leaned back in her seat and stared at the tiny reading light in the ceiling. She stifled a yawn and tried to work up enough energy to get a book out of her purse. She yawned again and decided to close her eyes and rest for a few minutes first. She really was tired. She'd been so excited last night that she'd barely slept, and her harried morning, combined with her enervating fear of flying, had completely drained what little energy reserves she had. She snuggled into a comfortable position and drifted off to sleep.

A sharp lurch penetrated Lucy's dreamless slumber, and when a screeching thump shook the plane her eyes flew open and she looked around in confusion.

"Take it easy. We're landing." Caleb's calm voice scattered the last remnants of her sleep.

"What happened?" Lucy's voice was strained as she grabbed his hand.

"Nothing happened, except that you've been snoring on my shoulder for the better part of three hours."

"I have not!" Lucy vehemently denied. "I don't snore."

"Well, maybe not a full-bodied snore," he conceded. "More like a series of small snuffles."

"I don't snuffle either!" Lucy insisted.

"Maybe I haven't got the right word," he suggested. "Tell you what, the next time you're asleep I'll tape the sound, and you can decide what to call it."

Lucy shot him a wary glance, barely noticing when the plane's thrust reversers came on. What was he trying to tell her? she wondered. That he found her desirable and intended to sleep with her again? Her body temperature shot up at the very thought. *Did* he find her desirable? She desperately wanted to know the answer to that particular question, but there was no way to find out. Even if she came right out and asked him, he would hardly tell her if he'd found her a disappointment in bed. Whatever else Caleb might be, he was essentially a very kind man. He'd never deal her a blow like that.

The disembarking instructions broke into her thoughts, and Lucy looked around in amazement. People were gathering up their things prior to leaving. Between her confusion at waking and Caleb's insults, she'd barely noticed the landing.

"You're lucky you slept through the whole flight," the woman beside her pronounced. "My nerves are much too delicate to ever sleep on a plane—as are poor Fou-Fou's." She smiled benevolently down at the carrier, which was now in her plump lap. "But your husband shouldn't have teased you about snoring. As for bringing a tape recorder into your bedroom . . ." She sniffed expressively.

"Oh, it's all right," Lucy answered, her mind still foggy with sleep, "we're not married."

"Not married!" The woman's eyes popped, and she shifted Fou-Fou's carrier further away from Lucy as if she expected her to contaminate the cat.

Lucy briefly closed her eyes, wishing she had the right to say they were lovers—but she didn't. Neither could she quite bring herself to be rude and tell the woman to mind her own business.

Before she could decide what to say, Caleb leaned across her and whispered confidentially, "Actually, she belongs to me. I picked her up in a bazaar in Marrakech. She makes a rather tempting addition to my harem, don't you think?"

Lucy gulped down laughter at the outrageous comment.

"Harem!" The woman's pale eyes bulged.

"Uh-huh." Caleb nodded seriously. "All us sheikhs have harems."

"Sheikhs?" The woman eyed Caleb suspiciously. "You don't look like any Arab I ever saw."

"That's because I'm not wearing my robes," he agreed.

"You're blond!" she accused.

"The Crusaders," Caleb said vaguely. "To say nothing of Lawrence of Arabia."

At a loss for an answer, the woman snorted and, using Fou-Fou's carrier as a wedge, forced herself into the stream of people moving down the aisle.

"Lawrence of Arabia?" Lucy couldn't contain her mirth.

"She deserved it," he said, frowning. "What we do is our own business."

Lucy grabbed her purse and they deplaned. She was still uncertain what to think of Caleb's exchange with the woman. Her program had given no indication that he liked to indulge in practical jokes—and further, she'd sensed his very real anger at the women's attitude. Lucy would have expected him to simply ignore it, not to get angry. Ah, well. Lucy filed the incident away to be examined later.

Caleb guided her into the busy airport.

"Where are we?" she asked curiously.

"Good God, woman, didn't you find out where I was taking you?"

Since she could hardly tell him that she scarcely cared where they were going as long as she was going with him, Lucy replied shortly, "I'm perfectly aware that we're going to Wyoming, but I didn't think the state had an airport this size."

"It doesn't," Caleb agreed as he steered her toward the baggage pickup area. "We're in Denver. You were still asleep when the pilot relayed that particular bit of information."

"Denver?" Lucy closed her eyes and tried to picture a map as Caleb grabbed their suitcases off the luggage carousel. Nothing materialized.

"We're south of Wyoming, and about two hundred and fifty miles from the resort." He frowned thoughtfully at her. Lucy, misunderstanding the reason, reached for her suitcase.

"You take my briefcase," he ordered. "I'll carry the bags."

"Okay." She obligingly took his work from under his arm. "What's wrong?" she demanded as he continued to frown.

"When I made these arrangements, I had my secretary charter a flight up to the resort."

"Chartered?" Lucy's stomach did a flip-flop. "As in

one of those tiny little things?"

"Afraid so," he answered, confirming her worst fears. "I didn't realize that you had such a thing about flying."

"Oh." Lucy's voice was hollow.

"Listen to me, Lucy. If you can't face a small plane, then we'll hire a car and drive up."

Lucy looked into his encouraging face, and her heart contracted with tenderness. He looked so tired, but despite his fatigue he was offering to undertake a five-hour drive over unfamiliar, mountainous roads simply to pander to her quite irrational fear of flying. She couldn't be so selfish.

"Nonsense," she said firmly. "I'd rather be scared for a forty-five-minute flight than wander around these mountains at night. Besides, Beth and Joel will be expecting us."

"You're sure?" Caleb's blue eyes searched her pale face, trying to read an answer.

"Positive. I may be a coward, but no one can say I'm not a game one."

"That's my Lucy." His voice seemed to caress her nerve endings, making her glow with pleasure at his approval. At that moment she would have agreed to fly the plane herself if he'd asked her. Fortunately, such a sacrifice wasn't demanded.

They located the charter company without any difficulty and within half an hour were airborne, heading north. To Lucy's amazement and Caleb's amusement, flying in the tiny, four-passenger craft wasn't at all alarming to her. Being able to watch the pilot as well as having a clear view out the windshield made it seem more like riding in a car than a plane.

Once they were actually in the air, Lucy looked around with pleasure. She felt like a bird. She studied the mountains to their left, rather impressed. The Rockies seemed so much rawer—to say nothing of higher—than the Adirondacks. Denver itself from the air was a bit of a surprise.

Lucy voiced her disappointment. "It's flat!"

"What is?"

"Denver. It's in the Rockies, so how can it be flat?"

"Denver's actually built on a plateau a mile up. The foothills of the Rockies don't really start until the extreme western suburbs. But for all that, it's a lovely city. Next time I'll show it to you." He turned back to the papers he was studying.

Lucy glowed inwardly at his casual reference to a next time. Did he mean that, or was it merely a comment to placate her—much like a man's saying "I'll call" when he has no intention of doing so? Even though she knew it was much more likely to be the latter, Lucy's tiny glow of happiness couldn't be entirely dimmed.

An hour later they landed, and were met at the airstrip by a car from the resort. Lucy glanced curiously around as they pulled up in front of the main lodge.

The weathered gray stones of the building seemed to blend in perfectly with the rugged landscape. She and Caleb entered through gleaming glass doors and approached the huge, horseshoe-shaped reception desk. Lucy studied a map of the resort as she waited for Caleb to register. The giant building they were in housed several restaurants, shops, a snack bar, conference rooms, and a laundry, as well as nearly two hundred rooms. Scattered about the resort's grounds were an assortment of small buildings that contained four to six rooms each. They seemed to have catered to every taste, Lucy thought as she read a list of the facilities available, ranging from racquetball to swimming.

"The horses are supposed to be excellent. Not your average hired hacks," Caleb commented from behind her. "I'll take you riding."

"Horses?" Lucy repeated, remembering the program's warning that Caleb Bannister's perfect woman could ride. Damn, she swore silently, why hadn't they remembered that a western resort would be bound to have horses? "We can't go riding. I'm allergic to horses," Lucy quickly lied—and then frowned as she realized her mistake. She should have said Beth was allergic to horses.

"Really?" Caleb arched an eyebrow and studied her flushed face intently, making her extremely nervous. She lied so seldom that she wasn't very good at it.

"But look," Lucy babbled on, anxious to change the subject, "they've got both an indoor and an outdoor track." She pointed to the map.

"I didn't realize you were so interested in running." His mouth quirked in amusement. "That exercise I taught you must have been more effective than I thought."

Lucy flushed as she remembered that exercise or, more specifically, the feel of his probing hands along the length of her leg.

"We'll have to run together," he added.

"Sure," Lucy agreed, thinking she must be out of her mind.

"Come on. I'll show you to your room so you can freshen up before we find Beth and Joel."

His eagerness to find Beth deflated Lucy, and she trailed along behind Caleb and the young bellhop who had their suitcases.

They left the main building and ambled down a flagstone path set in an emerald-green lawn. Her room was in a small building of gray stone, set far enough away from the recreational facilities so that there wouldn't be a constant stream of people past her door. Behind her building stretched the well-kept golf course.

The bellhop unlocked her door and set her suitcase inside.

"It's lovely," Lucy said honestly, liking the spaciousness of the room. A huge circular bed dominated the interior, but she barely noticed it. She was drawn to the sliding glass doors, which opened into a completely enclosed patio, the central focus of which was a hot tub.

Bannister had no trouble following the direction of her thoughts. "Give it a try. I'm going to settle in and then try to contact the others."

"Okay." Lucy replied awkwardly. She wanted to ask him where his room was, but the silent bellhop made her self-conscious, so she merely smiled as they left and then locked the door behind them.

CHAPTER
Ten

LUCY TOSSED HER blazer on the wide bed and stretched. She wasn't tired—her long nap had seen to that—but her muscles felt cramped and tight, like a watch that had been overwound. She hunched her back, wiggled her shoulders, and wandered out through the glass doors to inspect the patio.

It was small, no more than fifteen feet square, and paved in a heavy gray flagstone. A ten-foot-high redwood privacy fence completely walled it in. Immediately to the right of the sliding glass doors, a tall shrub had been planted in a redwood container. At its base were several small clay pots containing bright yellow mums. On the other side of the patio were two comfortable-looking loungers with a redwood table between them. But the hot tub dominated the small area.

Lucy studied it with interest. She'd never been in a hot tub before, and it looked inviting. Someone had obviously switched it on before they'd arrived, because Lucy could see a faint hint of steam hovering at surface level where the cooling mountain air met the heated water.

Lucy stretched again. A soak in a hot tub sounded heavenly, and much more refreshing than a quick shower. She frowned slightly as she considered what one wore to soak. A bathing suit? It seemed a shame to wet the only suit she'd brought when the tub couldn't have been any more private if it were located in the bathroom. The only way into the patio was through her room or over a ten-foot fence. Feeling suddenly daring, Lucy hurried back into her room. She doublechecked to make sure she'd locked the outer door and, after grabbing a large, fluffy towel from the bathroom, stripped off her clothes, flinging them onto the bed with carefree abandon.

It felt strange to walk outdoors without a stitch on, even though she knew no one but a bird could see her. It gave her a deliciously wicked feeling.

She climbed the three steps up to the tub and swung a bare leg over the side, grimacing as her foot felt the hot water. Cautiously, she inched the rest of her body down into the water while she tried to remember the caveats she'd read about hot tubs. All that came to mind was something about people with weak hearts. Shrugging, she sat down on the submerged bench and leaned back against the side. The water almost covered her breasts. She sighed blissfully at the exquisite sensations. No wonder California was so popular, if this was a sample of the delights to be found there. She lost track of the time as she sat there, her mind a peaceful blank and her body fast becoming a limp rag.

Her first intimation that she wasn't alone came when she heard an amused chuckle. She straightened suddenly and her eyes flew open. She was dumbfounded to see Caleb's tall form in the patio doorway.

"How did you get in here?" Lucy demanded, trying to gather her scattered wits. "I locked the door."

"And I unlocked it."

"How?" She frowned.

"With the key, of course," he said dryly. "The bellhop gave it to me. He assumed we were a pair, despite the separate rooms."

"Oh," she mumbled, her heart lifting at the thought of anyone linking them together. "Well, leave it here when you go. I don't like the idea of spare keys floating around." She was objecting only for form's sake—she had no intention of letting him know just how much she was willing to give him.

"Speaking of floating..." He walked out into the patio.

"Stay there!" she ordered. "I haven't got anything on. I didn't want to get my only swimsuit wet."

"I don't mind." He ignored her order and perched on the edge of the tub. His eyes darkened as they watched the water swirl around her breasts. "I've seen you in the bath before."

"That was different!" Lucy protested. "It was full of bubbles."

"Bubbles turn you on, do they?" he asked with a grin.

"Don't be—" Lucy's voice caught in her throat as he reached out a large hand and began tracing the water level around her breasts.

Lucy scrunched down on the seat as his fingers boldly cupped her soft flesh. His thumb began a flicking, teasing motion on the dusky pink tip until it hardened against his palm.

"Beth and Joel checked in right after lunch, and the clerk thinks they're out on the golf course. I left a message for them."

"That's nice," Lucy muttered, Caleb's words echoing meaninglessly in her mind. Nothing was registering except the touch of his fingers.

Suddenly, to her dismay, his hand was withdrawn and he straightened. Lucy looked up at him, her eyes so full of unconscious appeal that he smiled. He walked back toward the door, and Lucy swallowed her bitter disappointment. But he didn't leave as she'd expected. He stopped by the lounge and casually unstrapped his wristwatch, dropping it on the table. Then he sat down and slipped off his Adidas and thick gray athletic socks.

Lucy watched in fascination as he pulled his blue knit shirt over his head and dropped it on the lounger. Her eyes clung to his broad chest with its heavy mat of curly blond hair. Her fingers tingled as she remembered the feel of that hair against her hands.

"Enjoying yourself?" His tender smile tore at her heart.

"Why not?" She forced the words past the constriction in her throat. "Haven't you heard that male strippers are all the rage?"

"No," he replied dryly. "I can't say that it's come to my attention."

"That's probably because you'd much rather ogle women!"

"Woman, as in the singular." His eyes caressed her and promised pleasures to come.

Lucy watched as he unsnapped his silver belt buckle and unzipped his faded jeans. A quick movement of his wrists and they were off. Lucy hungrily drank in the sight of him, standing there in a brief pair of white shorts that did nothing to disguise his arousal.

She looked down at the water, unable to watch him shed the last trappings of civilization. Somehow her desire for him went deeper than merely a physical attraction, and she was afraid that the intensity of her feelings would show on her face. She wasn't all that sure she could handle her feelings herself. Later she would consider them, she promised herself, glancing up just in time to see one strongly muscled leg come over the edge of the tub.

"Are you going to soak, too?" Lucy asked and then blushed at the idiocy of the question. It was like asking a fox in the chicken coop if he were a vegetarian.

"Among other things." Caleb chuckled as he lowered himself into the water. "Ah, that feels good." He stretched, and Lucy watched as the muscles rippled across his chest. She gulped at the unexpected force of her desire. She wanted to touch his hard frame, to tease and torment him, to drive him completely out of his mind.

Why not? she asked herself. She wanted him. Why not make the first move? But she found it impossible to risk the consequences. If he rebuffed her, she'd curl up and die.

"What are you plotting now?" Caleb studied the fleeting emotions on her expressive face.

Lucy forced herself to meet his glowing eyes. She searched them. For what, she wasn't certain, but at least she found desire there. Hot and sure. Desire for her. Not for some green-eyed, five-foot-two blonde. The knowledge freed her fragile self-confidence, and she reached out a tentative hand to lightly stroke his chest. She ran her fingers over his flat masculine nipples, teasing them lightly with her nails.

He smiled lazily and Lucy grew bolder.

"You don't mind?" Lucy queried as her hand wandered down the arrow of his blond hair.

"Mind!" His voice was harsh. "Woman, you overestimate yourself. I can handle you."

"Are you sure?" Lucy tossed him a wicked look, challenged by his words. She desperately wanted to explore his body, to learn all its secrets, all its pleasure points. She wanted to drive him into the same type of frenzy he'd so easily created in her.

Hesitantly, she moved closer to him. The warm water swirled around her waist, its heat seeming to sensitize every part of her body. Tentatively, her hands went to his face and her fingers began lightly exploring his features, feeling the crevices of his ears, tracing the passionate curl of his lips, and sliding along his slightly scratchy jawline. Her fingers slipped down his neck, gently outlining the muscles and cords as she went.

Lucy sighed happily, all rational thought suspended as she indulged in the role of temptress—although the tingling sensation growing in her abdomen gave proof that she was as affected as he was.

She focused her attention on his chest, planting tiny kisses across his collarbone before slipping lower. Her lips tugged gently on his crisp hair, and she felt his body tremble in reaction.

"Nice," she murmured abstractedly. Her tongue licked his nipples. Remembering the pleasure he'd given her, she nipped them lightly with her teeth, taking immense satisfaction from the shudder which shook his powerful frame. She felt omnipotent. She, Lucy Travers, a five-ten Amazon, was the one slowly driving him out of his mind—not some dimwit, pint-sized blonde.

Boldly, her mouth strung kisses down his chest, pausing to explore his navel with her tongue.

"My God!" he gasped. "I think I've created a monster!"

Lucy gazed innocently up at him as her hands glided under the water and closed over the proof of her seductive efforts.

"I'm only human, woman, and you just pushed me past my limit." He reached down and lifted her out of the water, cradling her tingling body against him as he sat down on the submerged bench.

"What—" Lucy began, then gasped as he slipped a hand between her legs, using the buoyancy of the water and the pressure of his fingers to lever her upward.

"Now it's my turn, sweet temptress." His mouth closed over the hardened tip of her breast and she whimpered as the tugging pressure tightened the knot of desire in her loins.

"Caleb!" Her fingers fastened in his silky blond hair, clenching convulsively as he deepened the pressure. He lifted his head and regarded her other breast with passion-darkened eyes. He began teasing its taut point with his tongue and Lucy moaned in exquisite frustration. She shuddered, and her eyes flew open as the hand holding her out of the water began to move, stroking the very core of her sensitized femininity. Her face flushed and her lips parted; her breath was coming in short gasps. She shivered convulsively and strained to get closer to him.

"Please, Caleb," she begged. "Please, I need you." She had no thought of coyness. Somehow he had managed to strip away all the layers of doubts and social inhibitions to reveal her elemental need of him. She felt that if he didn't bring their lovemaking to its natural conclusion she'd go mad.

But instead of leaving the tub as she'd expected, he lifted her higher and then gently lowered her pliant body, filling the emptiness within her.

Lucy's eyes widened and for a moment his possession was sufficient. She arched back against his arms, quivering in satisfaction as his lips nuzzled her swollen breasts.

"Caleb," she said with a moan, "we'll drown!"

"But what a way to go." His laughter reverberated through her body, and Lucy absorbed the movement. "Actually..." The husky sound of his voice made her wiggle with pleasure, drawing an answering gasp from Caleb. "Actually," he tried again, "the logistics of this aren't impossible. We'll..." He looked up from the breast he was teasing into her flushed face. Her eyes were closed the better to concentrate on the hot, invading warmth of him.

"Lucy, are you listening to me?"

"No," she replied honestly. "At the moment I haven't the slightest interest in your mind."

"Of all the sexist remarks." He chuckled. "And here I thought you respected me."

"Caleb!" Lucy shook his massive shoulder. "This is not the time to get gabby!"

"Oh, and what time is it? Time for this?" He surged upward, and Lucy clutched at him, swept with a desire so strong it was almost unbearable.

"Yes, yes, yes!" she cried. "Stop tormenting me or—"

But she had no need to complete her threat as Caleb, too, reached the end of his endurance. He began to move, establishing a rhythmic pattern that reduced Lucy to a mindless sensual entity, the essence of feminine response, until finally, with one last powerful thrust of his body, he sent them both spinning into a fiery world of pure sensation.

Slowly, Lucy floated back to earth and opened her eyes to find herself cradled against his hair-roughened chest.

"Much as I hate to break up this delightful interlude, I'm afraid I'm going to have to. For one thing, you're going to have Beth on your doorstep shortly. And, for another, hot tubs should be used in moderation."

"Oh, dear." Lucy batted her eyelashes at him in a caricature of a coquette. "And you were so immoderate, too."

Caleb stood up, still holding her. He swung her over the side of the tub, depositing her dripping body on the flagstones.

"It's chilly," Lucy observed idly, watching as he vaulted lightly out of the tub. She didn't think she'd ever get tired of watching the incredible combination of bone and muscle that comprised his magnificent physique.

"Yes, and you've got goose bumps in the most intriguing spots." He leered engagingly at her.

"Fie, and aren't you the flatterer, sir!"

"Well"—Caleb picked up Lucy's towel and began to briskly rub his body dry—"in the interest of honesty, I'm not so sure that it is flattery. I mean, the goose bumps are rather fetching, especially the ones on your behind, but that shade of blue you're turning is definitely not you. It clashes with your carroty hair."

"Carroty hair!" Lucy was outraged. No one had dared to call her "Carrots" since the third grade, when she'd bloodied some boy's nose for the crime.

"Perhaps not carroty," he conceded. "More like a radish." He dropped the wet towel on the lounge and began to dress, giving her a serene smile totally belied by the glint of mischief in his eyes. "My own little radish-head. You were right to point it out." He pulled the shirt over his head. "Relationships have a much better chance to prosper if all the little annoyances can be worked out."

Lucy clamped down on her outrage, well aware of the futility of rising to his teasing. Instead, she returned his smile and gleefully wrapped her arms around him, rubbing her dripping body against his clothes. Radish-head, indeed!

"You're so right, Caleb," Lucy purred as she wiggled sideways so as to wipe the maximum amount of water off on him. "Lack of communication can wreak havoc on a relationship."

"So can lack of respect," he said ruefully as his arms encircled her, holding her immobile for a brief moment before he dropped a quick kiss on her lips. "How about if we compromise. I won't call you radish-head if you don't . . ." He paused as if trying to think of something.

"And I won't throw my wet body at you." Lucy stepped back and laughed at the damp imprint along his shirt front.

"Your understanding of the male mind is absolutely zero if you think that's an inducement for anything. As a matter of fact, it sounds more like a threat to me. I guess I'll just have to keep calling you radish-head," he said mournfully.

"You'll do it at the risk of your life and limb," Lucy threatened and then shivered as a cool breeze wafted over her wet back.

"Inside, Lucy." Caleb lost all resemblance to a teasing lover and became his usual brisk self. "You're not used to how quickly the air cools off up here in the Rockies once the sun sets. Go get dressed. I'll meet you in the lounge for dinner in about half an hour. Now, move!" He accompanied the order with a gentle smack on her rump.

Lucy hurried into the bathroom and, grabbing another oversized towel, began to rub herself dry. Standing there flirting with him, she hadn't realized just how cold it was getting. As she tossed the damp towel over the drying rack, she heard the outside door slam behind him. She closed her eyes for a moment, reliving the scene in the hot tub.

She chewed her lower lip as she remembered her

wantonly aggressive behavior. What had he really thought about it? Especially considering that his own tastes ran toward the ultimate in docile femininity?

He'd implied that feminine aggression didn't bother him, but Lucy was mature enough to know that men were liable to do or say anything in the throes of passion. That was not a reliable indicator of anything except, perhaps, a momentary desire for sex. And he'd finally resumed control of their lovemaking, Lucy remembered, wondering if he'd done it because he'd been disgusted with her forwardness or merely because he'd wanted to.

So what did she care? Lucy demanded of her tousled reflection in the mirror. The answer percolated into her mind from somewhere deep in her subconscious. She cared because she loved him.

No! Lucy protested inwardly. *No, I can't love him!* She leaned her head against the cold mirror. Surely fate couldn't be so unkind. But it had been. Somewhere between being rescued from a fat Pekingese and burning her mouth on beef in black bean sauce, she'd tumbled headlong into love.

Perhaps she was merely infatuated with him, she told herself. After all, he certainly had all the prerequisites. He was rich, powerful, built like a Greek god, and made love like a romantic fantasy. But she knew too much about Caleb Bannister to be infatuated with him. Thanks to her program, she knew facets of his life he'd probably forgotten himself. And while he was undeniably powerful, she knew nothing about high finance and cared even less, so his ability to manipulate it didn't really impress her. As for his money . . . Lucy frowned. It didn't really seem to be a factor in their relationship. Granted it was there, but he hadn't lavishly spread money around. His gift of the chocolates had been tasteful rather than ostentatious. And while his tailoring was exquisite, Lucy knew salesmen who dressed just as well, as part and parcel of their jobs. Even this resort, lovely as it was, wasn't beyond her own means.

No, Lucy sighed unhappily. It was Caleb Bannister himself whom she loved, the engaging man who lived behind the rich and powerful tag. The man who jogged around the park half-naked, rescuing ill-prepared runners. The man who wolfed down cartons of hot food, made love like an expert, and teased her about the color of her hair. That was the man she loved—for all the good it would do her.

She gulped down an immature desire to burst into tears. He'd never said a single word about love even when they'd been making love.

So how did he feel about her? Lucy worried the question around in her mind. He definitely liked her. He liked to talk to her, to tease her, and occasionally to go to bed with her. But that hardly added up to his being in love with her. Only a totally naive woman could be so stupid as to assume that a man loved her simply because he made love to her. Men, even the best of them, were quite willing to take whatever was offered. And she'd certainly offered. She remembered her behavior in the hot tub in dismay. She'd not only offered, she'd practically demanded.

Stop it! She tried to suppress her tortured thoughts. She didn't know what Caleb thought. Besides, no matter why he made love to her, he enjoyed it. The indisputable fact gave her some slight satisfaction.

But the memory of Beth brought her mind up short again as she considered her friend's continued determination to marry Bannister. Beth was really a side issue, Lucy admitted. Lucy would never attempt to steal a friend's lover, but in no way could Caleb be considered Beth's property. It was true that Beth was the living embodiment of his ideal woman. It was equally true that several things he'd said had given Lucy the idea that he had serious intentions about Beth, but for some reason he was biding his time before declaring himself. Still, the fact remained that Caleb had made no attempt to stake a claim on Beth, despite her obvious receptiveness to such a move.

Lucy remembered that their invitation to Wyoming had come from Joel, not Caleb—although Lucy had not the slightest doubt that if Caleb had not wanted them to come, they would have been excluded. Joel needed Caleb's goodwill too much to risk angering him.

Besides, if he was interested in Beth, why would he go to bed with Lucy? Because some men wouldn't dream of having sex with a woman they had serious intentions about. The answer made her faintly nauseated and she dropped her hairbrush in disgust. This had to stop. She was tying herself into knots, and it was all supposition.

A knock at the door distracted her, and she went to answer it, repeating one of Marcus's maxims: Respond to what you know to be fact, not to what you suspect might be. Lucy was able to greet Beth in her usual friendly manner, sincerely admiring Beth's gorgeous cowgirl outfit, complete with hand-tooled leather boots and fringed leather jacket.

"I bought it at that boutique off the main lobby." Beth stuck out a tiny foot the better to show off the elaborate designs on the boots. "Or rather, I charged it." She giggled. "That much money I didn't have on me. I'm hoping it will give Caleb ideas."

"It's more likely to give him ideas about horses," Lucy said dryly. "There are stables here."

"I figured that." Beth fell into step beside Lucy as they walked toward the dining room. "Maybe I should have stuck to a more conventional outfit like the one you've got on." She eyed Lucy approvingly.

"Thank you." Lucy glanced down at her trim figure almost in surprise. She'd been so overwhelmed by the unwelcome knowledge of her love for Caleb that she'd dressed in the first thing that had come to hand—her pants suit. For all she remembered, she could be wearing her nightgown.

"How was the flight?" Beth's eyes gleamed with interest. "I was really torn when Joel called and explained that Caleb was stuck in New York City until after lunch. I envied you the chance to have Caleb to yourself for the whole flight."

"I wouldn't have minded switching with you," Lucy lied.

"Well, I couldn't reach you to ask and, besides, the thought of trying to make conversation with Caleb for that long scared me to death." Beth grimaced. "How'd you do it?"

"I didn't." Lucy laughed, her normally happy spirits starting to resurface. "I fell asleep somewhere over Hoboken and didn't wake up until we touched down in Denver."

"You missed everything," Beth scolded. "It was a lovely flight. Joel and I had lots of fun."

"Beth . . ." Lucy paused at the imposing entrance to the main lobby. "Why don't you try to capture Joel instead of Caleb? It'd be a snap. The man's already head over heels in love with you."

"I'll tell you why," Beth responded instantly. "Because he's determined to sink every penny he owns into those gas wells of his. He's already mortgaged his ranch to the hilt, and it still wasn't enough. That's why he needs Caleb to find him a backer. I told you once before, if I'm going to have to learn to love a man after I marry him, then it's going to be a rich man."

"It's your life." Lucy sighed, wishing not for the first time that she'd never gotten involved in this fiasco. "Come on. Let's find the men. I haven't eaten since breakfast, and I'm starved."

They opted for the casual Rustler's Lounge. Lucy sank into the chair Caleb held for her and looked around with interest. The restaurant was filled with businessmen attending a conference being held at the resort. They outnumbered the women present by at least twenty to one. Lucy noticed the stares Beth was getting, and she glanced curiously at Caleb, wondering if he'd seen, too, but he was busy studying the menu.

Lucy listened to the men's conversation as she waited for dinner to be served. She perked up when the waitress, a charming college-aged woman dressed in an abbreviated version of a cowgirl outfit, served their salads—huge bowls of crisp lettuce dotted with fresh vegetables.

"Here's another radish for you, Lucy." Caleb dropped one in the middle of her salad, where it gleamed like the cherry on top of a sundae. "Lucy's much fonder of radishes than carrots," he blandly informed Beth and Joel.

"Thank you!" Lucy glared at him.

Beth glanced curiously from Caleb to Lucy, wondering at her friend's acid tone, but Caleb's charming smile reassured her.

"You can have mine too, Lucy," she offered. "I'm not all that fond of radishes."

"Thanks anyway, but I've had enough." Lucy shot Caleb a furious glance. The wretch!

"Mr. Bannister"—the waitress smiled at him—"there's a phone call for you at the desk."

"Thank you." He smiled at the young woman, then at the group. "I'll be right back."

"Probably someone else who needs money," Joel said disconsolately.

"Don't worry," Beth began and then sneezed.

"Bless you," Lucy said automatically. She frowned slightly as Beth kept her head bent over her salad.

"Oh, dear." Beth's voice sounded faint. "I think I'm getting a cold. Joel"—she addressed the tablecloth—"would you be a dear and get me a pack of tissues?"

"From where?" He looked around as if he expected one to materialize out of the woodwork.

"At the desk, please?" Beth begged prettily.

Joel obediently got to his feet and left.

"Lucy!" Beth looked up, her face horrified. "My contact came out when I sneezed!"

"Oh lord," Lucy looked into Beth's eyes. Sure enough,

one was a brilliant green and the other a plain blue.

"It fell into my salad!" Beth wailed. "What are we going to do? If Caleb sees me, our plans are shot."

Despite Lucy's private opinion that it might be for the best, she was unable to resist the appeal in Beth's multicolored eyes.

Joel returned much too soon with a small pack of Kleenex. "Here you are. The desk had loads."

"Thank you." Beth snatched one and held it in front of her face while she shot an imploring look at Lucy.

There was no way they were going to escape gracefully, Lucy realized, so they might as well escape speedily.

"Poor Beth, she does so suffer from colds," Lucy said to the confused Joel. "There's nothing you can do but put her to bed and let her sleep it off."

"But supper?" Joel said.

"You're right. She might get hungry later." Lucy signaled their waitress and requested a doggie bag, which the woman produced from a coffee stand against the far wall. "We'll just take her salad with us," Lucy chatted inanely. She tipped Beth's salad into the waxed bag and frowned at the amount of dressing left in the bottom of the bowl. The contact could be stuck in it. Trying to act as if she did this kind of thing all the time, Lucy nonchalantly used her napkin to wipe the bowl clean, then tossed the napkin in after the salad while Joel watched in horror. "There, you have a salad to eat later," Lucy informed Beth, who peeped up at her with one green eye. "Let's go."

"But you can't!" Joel tried.

"Don't want her to get sick, you know." Lucy gave him a vacuous smile and hurried along behind Beth, who, from the sight of her shaking shoulders, was having difficulty restraining her mirth.

Once they were safely outside, Beth went off into peals of laughter. "Oh, Lucy, if only you could have seen Joel's face when you calmly wiped out the salad bowl and tossed the napkin in!"

"Why is it," Lucy demanded, "that whenever you do something dumb, *I'm* the one who winds up looking like a fool?"

"Never mind," Beth consoled her. "Unless"—the idea had obviously just occurred to her—"you fancy Joel?"

"Lord, no!" Lucy's voice left no room for doubt. "But that still doesn't mean that I want him to think I'm some kind of nut—and God only knows what Caleb will think when he comes back and we aren't there."

"Don't worry. Joel will tell him what happened."

"That's what I'm afraid of," Lucy said tartly. "Come on. Let's play hunt the contact, then order dinner from room service. I'm starved."

"Okay." Beth began to giggle again.

CHAPTER
Eleven

LUCY STUDIED HER reflection in her bedroom mirror. Worn denims covered her long legs, and she wore a plain white cotton shirt topped by a blue sweat shirt with a faded Columbia University emblem imprinted across the front. She had braided her long hair into a single shining rope.

Right after breakfast, she and Beth were going to accompany the men into the mountains to look over Joel's gas well site. They had been instructed to dress practically. The trouble was, Lucy didn't have the vaguest idea what constituted "practical" in this situation. She'd never traipsed through the mountains in her life—nor wanted to, for that matter. Central Park was as close to nature as she cared to get.

A brisk knock on the door sounded, and Lucy padded across the heavy plush carpet to open it. A maid wearing the resort's distinctive burgundy-and-gold uniform stood in the doorway holding a tray.

"Come in." Lucy eyed the steaming pot of coffee appreciatively. She never felt fully human until after her second cup in the morning. "Just set it there." Lucy pointed to the empty desk top. "It certainly is nice of the resort to provide early-morning coffee."

"Oh, it wasn't the resort," the woman said candidly as she set the tray down. "It was that gorgeous blond hunk in 11-C."

"You mean Mr. Bannister?" Lucy warmed at the small sign of Caleb's consideration.

"That's the one." The woman chuckled. "What I

wouldn't give to be twenty years younger. Not that I'd stand much of a chance—not considering the way his interests lie."

Lucy bent over her purse in embarrassment as she rummaged in the bottom for a tip. She wondered if the woman had somehow found out what had happened in her hot tub the day before. But the maid's next words made it only too clear that she'd never given a thought to Lucy's being romantically involved with the "hunk."

"Yup. I was taking a drink over to 9-C about one-thirty this morning when I saw the most gorgeous little blonde leaving his room. If they didn't look a picture there in the doorway." The woman sighed romantically. "Him so big and her no more than heart high."

Lucy's purse dropped from her suddenly slack fingers, and she stared down at it as if she'd never seen it before. She could feel her face pale and stiffen, and her stomach suddenly became a lead weight.

"Are you okay, miss?" The maid looked curiously at her. She had no idea of the magnitude of the blow she'd just delivered, and that compounded Lucy's hurt. Apparently her computer wasn't the only one capable of accurately assessing Caleb's tastes—even the maid corroborated the program.

"I didn't mean to shock you. It's just so commonplace to me. If you knew what I've seen!" She rolled her eyes suggestively.

"I can imagine." Lucy forced a strained smile. She grabbed a bill and shoved it at the woman, closing the door behind her.

You are not going to cry! she told herself fiercely. It wouldn't help a thing. Besides, her face would be a swollen mess, and they would know she'd been bawling.

That thought, more than any other, strengthened her resolve, and she glared at the coffee tray. Her appetite had suddenly deserted her, and she eyed the cherry Danish with distaste.

What had happened after she had helped Beth find

the missing contact and had gone to her room for the
night? Beth hadn't said anything about rejoining the men.
Lucy had merely assumed that Beth wasn't going to. But
she must have. Lucy shook her head in confusion. Right
before dinner, Beth had said she was glad she hadn't had
to fly out with Caleb because she had trouble talking to
him. But then, maybe they weren't interested in talk.
She knew from experience that conversation wasn't necessary for what they'd obviously done.

But why had it happened? Lucy searched her mind
for a clue without success. She'd known all along that
Beth was Caleb's fantasy woman, but he hadn't seemed
inclined to declare himself. So why had he suddenly
decided to stake a claim by the very basic method of
taking Beth to bed? Had Joel's obvious infatuation with
Beth pushed him into showing his hand sooner than he'd
wanted to? But why sneak around in the middle of the
night? Caleb wasn't afraid of Joel—Joel was the one
needing help. Unless Caleb felt the need to make sure
of Beth, but didn't want to hurt Lucy more than nec-
cesary. Could he possibly have realized just how much
she loved him? Maybe he wanted to let her down easily—
but not at the risk of losing Beth to Joel.

Lucy chewed on her lower lip. What if he'd told Beth
about their lovemaking?

The tiny travel alarm went off, signifying that it was
time to join the others in the dining room. Lucy automatically shut it off. She shrank from the thought of
facing Beth and Caleb, unable to bear the pity that would
be in their eyes at the idea that she could ever have been
so stupid as to have hoped to compete with Beth for
Caleb. It would have been a foolish hope at any time,
Lucy acknowledged without rancor, but knowing what
the computer had said, she must have been temporarily
insane to have even considered it.

Fortunately, her pride came to her rescue. She wasn't
going to hide in her room and go into a decline like some
rejected Victorian heroine.

So she'd been stupid enough to fall in love with him. So what! She wasn't the first woman to make a fool of herself over him, and she wouldn't be the last. Next month he probably wouldn't even remember her. But that thought merely made her want to cry again. At least he didn't know how she felt, she encouraged herself as she slipped into her running shoes and prepared to face them.

Lucy found the three of them seated at a table in the dining room. She gave them a bright, meaningless smile and slipped into the seat Caleb held for her, hating her treacherous body for the way it quickened to life when his hand brushed casually across her back.

"Hi, Lucy." Beth gave her an uncertain smile.

Lucy held on to her composure only with an extreme effort. She knew Beth well enough to have no trouble interpreting that look. It held confusion and apology. Caleb must have confessed his dalliance with her to Beth. For one brief moment Lucy hated him with a fierce anger. Why couldn't he have at least kept his mouth shut!

"I already ordered for you." Caleb gave her a cheerful smile that made Lucy long to smack him. He had no idea just how badly he'd hurt her. Or else he simply didn't care. Well, if he could act as if nothing had happened, so could she. He wasn't going to remember her as a whining, crying female—provided that he remembered her at all.

"Sorry to be late. I got waylaid." She became fascinated with putting cream and sugar in her coffee, missing Caleb's narrowed stare.

"At least you're dressed appropriately," Joel commented. "Flat shoes and long sleeves are a must in the mountains."

"Are we planning on hiking?" Lucy asked indifferently. She doubted she would care if he told her they were about to cross the Continental Divide on foot.

"Not if I can help it," Beth denied. "That crack about being dressed appropriately was aimed at me, Lucy. He took exception to my cowboy boots, but I'm not going to change them." Beth tossed her curly blond hair challengingly.

Joel opened his mouth for a pithy observation—if the thunderous expression on his face was anything to go by—but fortunately the waitress brought their food.

Lucy stared blankly down at her plate, her stomach rebelling at the sight of the scrambled eggs, sausage, home fried, and muffins. She knew with dreadful certainty that if she ate that, she'd disgrace herself by being sick. She pushed the plate away and picked up her coffee cup.

"If you don't want eggs, may I order something else for you?" Caleb asked.

Lucy forced herself to meet his bright blue gaze, wishing she could believe that the faint concern she saw there was for her. More likely he was worried that she might make a scene once she found out about him and Beth.

"No, thanks, I had something in my room," Lucy lied.

"As you wish." He motioned to the waitress to remove Lucy's plate. "We're taking a picnic lunch with us, so if you get hungry you can raid it."

"All right," Lucy managed to say, wishing that he'd simply ignore her. His pseudo-concern was destroying her defenses.

Lucy retreated into herself, silently sipping her coffee. Not that the others seemed to notice her withdrawal. Beth took the conversation in her capable little hands and kept it there. At least last night had accomplished one thing, Lucy noted cynically. Beth was no longer wary of Caleb Bannister. Now she smiled quite naturally at him. Nor was she willing to give up her hold on Joel. Lucy watched as Beth continued to flirt outrageously with the rancher. Caleb's indulgent expression as he listened to Beth surprised Lucy. The computer had been wrong about one thing—Bannister was not a jealous lover.

After what seemed like hours, the others finally finished eating. Lucy trailed along behind them out into the parking lot, where Caleb walked toward a battered-looking jeep.

Lucy took a malicious pleasure in the fact that he seated Beth in the back, while Joel climbed into the front.

"Quit daydreaming, Lucy!" Caleb said to her. She hurriedly started to climb into the rear beside Beth, almost losing her balance when Caleb's hand slid across her hips in a suggestive caress. Lucy glanced quickly at Beth and Joel, but they'd missed it. She turned to glare at Caleb, who gave her a smile of such charming innocence that, if she hadn't felt her entire body react to his touch, she would have thought she'd imagined his caress. But she had felt it, and she distrusted that angelic expression. God only knew what he was planning behind it. Surely he didn't expect to carry on with both of them! To Lucy's shame, for one wild moment she actually considered it, before she clamped her lips together and refused to look at him. Her outrage was directed as much against herself as against him.

Lucy rode in the back, oblivious to the beauty of the austere landscape. She barely noticed when they began to climb into the foothills. Beth's gasps of alarm at the sheer drops alongside the unprotected road never even penetrated her gloom. Neither did the sharp glances Caleb gave her in the rear-view mirror.

One and a half interminable hours later, Caleb pulled the jeep onto the narrow shoulder and cut the engine.

Lucy roused herself slightly as she noticed the absolutely straight pine trees and asked what they were.

"Lodgepole pines," Joel answered absently as he unfolded what looked like, to Lucy's inexperienced eyes, a surveyor's map. "They grow absolutely straight, and the Indians used to use them as tent poles, hence the name."

"I see," Lucy murmured inanely, but Joel had already

forgotten her in his perusal of the map.

"The site's about three miles over that ridge." Joel pointed toward what appeared to Lucy to be a completely impenetrable area. There were no roads and the trees grew thickly.

"Uh-huh," Caleb agreed after looking at the map. "Coming?" he invited the two women.

"Not on your life!" Beth snapped. "I have no interest in chasing pipe dreams. Lucy and I will stay here. Right, Lucy?"

"Okay," Lucy agreed listlessly. She didn't particularly want to stay with Beth, but even less did she want to go with Caleb.

"Please yourself," Joel said stiffly, starting up the trail.

"You two stay within sight of the jeep," Caleb ordered, not making the slightest attempt to disguise his order as a suggestion. "People get lost up here every summer, and it's a race to find them before they fall off a cliff or get bitten by a rattler."

"Snakes!" Beth's green eyes widened and she darted an apprehensive glance toward the ground. "Don't worry. I'm not going anywhere!" She shivered expressively.

"We'll be back in a couple of hours. If you get hungry, there's food and drink in the picnic hamper. Help yourself. I had them pack extra," Caleb said.

"Thank you." Lucy aimed her words over his left shoulder, not meeting his eyes.

Caleb gritted his teeth in frustration, and for a moment Lucy was afraid he was going to comment on her surly attitude, but Joel's shout from halfway up the hill stopped him. With a look at Lucy that promised retribution later, he shouldered his back pack and left.

"God, I'm tired." Beth stretched. "I feel like I haven't slept in a week. This time difference is hell."

That and having Caleb make love to you until one-thirty in the morning, Lucy thought sourly.

"You must be tired, too, Lucy. It isn't like you to be so touchy. How about if we take a nap? I'll flip you for who gets the back seat."

"You can have it, Beth. I'm not sleepy. I'd rather stretch my legs a little."

"Okay." Beth promptly curled up on the warm vinyl, adding, "But don't get lost. The thought of trying to explain to Caleb why you disregarded his instructions is more than I care to contemplate."

"Don't worry. I'm not the adventurous type. I'll just follow the road a ways and then come back." Lucy jumped out of the jeep and started out at a brisk pace, hoping that the crisp mountain air and the magnificent scenery would give her something to concentrate on besides her own tortured thoughts. It didn't. About a quarter of a mile up the road, she sat down on a good-sized stump beside a particularly nasty-looking dropoff, and sluggishly shook the pebbles out of her shoes.

Lucy, you're a fool, she told herself, unable to hold back the tears that seeped out from behind her closed lids. She'd known all the time that she was playing with fire. That was the unforgivable part. If she'd had an ounce of common sense, she would have avoided Caleb like the plague once she'd read that computer printout. It was obvious from the beginning that nothing would ever come of her fling with him. It was simply that she hadn't expected the nothing to come so quickly. She'd hoped to have some time with him first. Then, too, she'd never expected to fall in love with him.

She wiped the streaming tears away with a careless hand. What now? She didn't really have a lot of choice. She could either accept what had happened and go on from there, or she could wallow in self-pity, acting like a spoiled child. At least she knew she could fall in love, she thought a trifle hysterically. Maybe she should write her own program and find herself a man who went in for Amazons instead of the pocket Venus type.

Lucy chuckled tearily as she saw herself writing program after program, trying to find a candidate. Ah, well, no one ever died of a broken heart. She stood up and stretched.

"Lucy!" Beth's sharp voice startled her and she jumped. Unfortunately, she also lost her balance.

"Lucy!" Beth screamed as Lucy swung her arms wildly in an attempt to regain her balance. With a muffled curse, she tumbled down the ravine. Vaguely in the distance she could hear Beth screaming, until the painful contact of her head with a large boulder abruptly silenced the sound.

"Lucy, Lucy!" The shaking on her shoulder jarred her throbbing head. Lucy moaned in protest.

"Lucy, are you dead?" Beth's shrieks sliced through Lucy's aching head like a dull knife.

"No, but you will be if you don't shut up," Lucy replied irritably. "My head hurts." She levered herself up, closing her eyes as the world tilted.

"You're hurt!" Beth cried.

"What was your first clue, Sherlock?" Lucy snapped, trying to wipe away the blood dripping into her left eye.

"It's all my fault," Beth said with a moan.

"Yes, it was!" Lucy agreed. She tried to stand, but her legs didn't seem to be obeying orders.

"Don't move." Beth jumped up. "I'll go get the jeep and then I'll help you up the hill."

"You do that." Lucy leaned back against the rocky ground, ready to agree with anything that would bring her a few minutes of peace and quiet.

She closed her eyes and drifted until the chugging sound of an engine penetrated her daze. She frowned slightly and forced her eyes open, blinking against the brilliant glare of the sun. She watched as the nose of the jeep peeped over the edge of the ravine. It came to a halt, then took a huge leap like a startled kangaroo. Beth's screams coincided with Lucy's realization that the jeep was teetering on the edge. Lucy watched in detached interest as the law of gravity won and the vehicle tumbled into the ravine.

Dimly, she realized that she should move, but it seemed like such a lot of trouble. By the time she'd mobilized her foggy mind, the jeep had plunged past her, coming to rest against a huge boulder about twenty-five feet farther down the gully.

"Lucy!" Beth scrambled down the slope, showering her friend with tiny rocks and twigs. "Did it hit you?"

"No," Lucy replied, "but you know, Beth, you didn't have to bring it as close as this."

"Oh, Lucy!" Beth broke into hysterical sobs. "I'm sorry. I've never driven a stick shift, and I didn't expect it to jump like that when I took my foot off the clutch."

"Live and learn," Lucy said wearily.

"Are you hysterical?" Beth gasped.

"No!" she replied tartly. "You're hysterical. I'm injured. Let's keep the players in this farce straight. Now do me a favor and check the jeep to see if you can smell gas."

"Why?" Beth stopped moaning long enough to ask.

"Because I don't have the slightest desire to end up as a pyrotechnical display!" Lucy snapped.

"Oh, I forgot about fire," Beth replied anxiously. "I'll go check."

She was back in a few minutes. "There's no leaking gas, so I used the CB to call the resort and tell them what happened."

"I see you rescued the picnic basket, too." Lucy commented. "Did all that screaming give you an appetite?"

"Lucy," Beth said, sniffing, "don't be mad."

"What did the resort say?" Lucy ignored the bid for sympathy.

"They're sending a car out after us right away. Uh . . . Lucy, I told them the brakes failed." She shot an imploring glance at her friend.

"I'm not going to tell them any differently," Lucy

said, "but I wouldn't count on them not eventually figuring out what happened."

"Maybe," Beth replied more cheerfully, "but even if they do, I'll be back in New York by then. And I'd much rather be yelled at by letter than in person."

"True." Lucy shifted slightly to move a rock from under her ribs.

"Hey! Look what I found." Beth pulled two bottles out of the basket. "Wine! We can use it to wash your cut."

"Not my cut you won't," Lucy objected.

"I once saw a movie where the hero had to do an emergency amputation, and he used brandy as the antiseptic."

"I once saw a movie where the Blob devoured Cleveland, but that doesn't mean I believe it. Let me have one of those bottles."

"What are you going to do with it?" Beth obligingly opened the wine and passed it to Lucy.

"Strange as it may seem, I intend to drink it." Lucy cautiously propped herself against a rock. She took a generous swallow. It wasn't bad. As a matter of fact, by the time Lucy had polished off the better part of the bottle, she thought it was excellent. The pain in her head had become a dull, disembodied ache and her various cuts, scrapes, and bruises seemed to have miraculously disappeared.

Beth, after weakly trying to dissuade Lucy from drinking so much, had sank down beside her to wait to be rescued.

Lucy was happily making inroads into the second bottle when she heard a faint shout.

"Wake up, Beth." Lucy poked the dozing Beth with the bottom of the half-empty wine bottle. "We've got company." She blinked, trying to clear her vision.

Beth let out a shriek that made Lucy moan, and almost immediately two men appeared over the edge of the ravine: Caleb and Joel.

Lucy muttered nastily as their hasty descent started a miniature avalanche of twigs and pebbles. She took another swallow of wine.

"What the hell do you think you're doing!" Caleb's furious words weren't so much a question as an accusation.

"I should think it's fairly obvious," Lucy snapped. "I'm drinking myself into oblivion, and a hard time I'm having of it. That's the second bottle, and I'm still not totally numb."

"It takes longer with wine." Caleb removed the bottle from her grasp. "Would you mind telling me just what the jeep is doing down here when I left it up there?"

"It's your own fault," Lucy said querulously. "If you were as smart as you think you are, you'd have taken the keys."

"One more time, Lucy. Why is the jeep down here?" She heard poor Beth's frightened gasp from behind her.

"I was trying to move it and I missed the curve." Lucy uncaringly took the blame. What difference did it make? Her heart was broken, to say nothing of her head. Why not leave Beth to her dreams. Lucy broke into self-pitying tears.

"Stop sniffling." Caleb's brusqueness was belied by the exquisite gentleness of his hands as he ran them over her limbs looking for breaks.

"Lucy!" He demanded her attention.

She tried to focus on his face. He seemed curiously pale, some detached part of her mind registered. He must have been worried about Beth. His vulnerability tore at her heart and she wanted to comfort him.

"Beth's fine," she muttered.

"Lucy," he said impatiently, "are you confused because of the wine you drank or because of the crack on your head?"

"I am not confused." She enunciated each word quite clearly. "I only drank the wine because my head hurt."

"Does it still hurt?" His fingers gently probed her scalp.

"Nothing hurts." She giggled happily. "Things stopped hurting halfway through the first bottle." She sighed. Even when she was half-drunk and covered with bruises, his touch could still reduce her to mindless pleasure.

"Oh, hell!" Caleb sounded exasperated. "There's no talking to a giggly drunk."

Almost on cue, the sound of a car motor broke the quiet, and Lucy giggled again. "Hark, the cavalry approaches."

The car came to a shrieking halt, and Lucy winced as the sound of the door slamming reverberated through her head.

"Poor Lucy." Caleb ran a gentle hand down her flushed face.

Lucy closed her eyes, moaning as his arms closed gently around her. Suddenly she realized he was picking her up.

"What are you doing?" she demanded.

"Carrying you up to the car."

"Don't be ridiculous," she protested. "You can't carry me up that slope. I'm five-ten and I weigh . . . well, never mind what I weigh. Remember what happened with the staircase."

Caleb ignored her and began to gingerly climb up to the road. Lucy squinted as the sun reflected off the gleaming white luxury car parked beside the dropoff. The glare made her head start pounding. She closed her eyes and hid her face in Caleb's shoulder.

Vague words like "insurance" and "liability" floated around her, and Lucy sniffed disconsolately, wondering whether the hotel would hold her responsible for the cost of the wrecked jeep. That would be the final straw. She rubbed her nose into Caleb's neck, breathing deeply of the smell of sun, soap, and clean masculine sweat. Its erotic effect penetrated even her wine-numbed senses, and she idly nibbled his ear.

"Later, Lucy," he whispered and she felt a chuckle ripple through his body.

Later, indeed! Later he'd be busy with Beth.

Caleb shifted her weight, and she found herself inside the car, sitting on his lap. He held her firmly in his arms as the car maneuvered to turn and began its swift journey back the way they had come.

Lucy heard Beth and Joel talking quietly in the front seat. She knew she ought to try to convince Caleb that she was perfectly capable of sitting up alone so that he could sit with Beth, but she wasn't that unselfish. This would probably be her last chance to be held close to him, to feel his hands on her. Beth would have him for the rest of her life. Surely she wouldn't begrudge Lucy this moment out of time.

The car swung sharply to the right, throwing Lucy back against Caleb. Remembering her supposed status as an invalid, she gave a soft little moan—something that wasn't hard to do. Between the thump on her skull, her overenthusiastic consumption of the wine, and her own miserable thoughts, her head suddenly felt as if it were about to come off.

"Try to relax, Lucy." Caleb's fingers gently rubbed the nape of her neck. Lucy sighed, subsiding in happy bonelessness against him, refusing to think beyond this moment.

CHAPTER
Twelve

THE CAR'S SUDDEN stop roused Lucy from her light doze. She snuggled deeper into Caleb's embrace, unwilling to wake up.

"Lucy!" Beth's worried voice demanded. "Are you all right?"

"Of course I'm all right," Lucy mumbled, accepting the inevitable. She could hardly blame Beth for wanting her awake and out of Caleb's arms. If their situations had been reversed, she would have been jealous, too.

"You sure don't look it." Joel's tone was faintly critical. "You should have had better sense than to try to drive a car you knew nothing about."

Joel's opinion mattered not one jot to Lucy. She could even find it in her heart to feel sorry for him. He'd lost the one he loved, too, even if he didn't know it yet.

The driver opened the back door, and Lucy took his hand, carefully climbing out. She straightened painfully as the hundreds of tiny scratches and bruises protested simultaneously.

"Thank you for the rescue." Lucy smiled at the driver and offered him her hand, only to withdraw it when she noticed the dirt and dried blood that clung to it. "Sorry, it's just surface gore."

"If you say so, miss." He clearly wasn't convinced. "If you need anything, feel free to call the desk," he told her as he handed the car keys to Caleb.

"I'm surprised he's willing to trust us with another car," Lucy said with a smile.

"I wasn't the one who wrecked the last one," Caleb pointed out.

Neither was I, Lucy almost answered, but she firmly bit down the words. There was no reason to implicate Beth at this point. Let him continue to think Beth perfect.

"Gather your wits and let's get moving," Caleb said.

"Certainly." Lucy automatically straightened at his tone. She began to move around the car toward the back of the building. She had no desire to traipse through the lobby looking like a refugee from an avalanche.

"All I need is a shower and a good long soak in the hot tub," Lucy stated—then winced as she remembered what had happened the last time she'd been in the hot tub. She shot a hesitant glance at Caleb, but he didn't seem to have heard her. He leaned over and opened the car door on the passenger's side.

"Get in." He gently bundled her into the front, buckling her in.

Lucy pressed herself back into the seat, trying to escape the warm heat from his body and the tantalizing scent of after shave that teased her nostrils. His hand brushed lightly against her breast, and Lucy's breath caught at the flood of sensual desire that tore through her.

"Sorry," he apologized, apparently thinking he'd touched a bruise.

"Don't be." Lucy sighed, keeping her gaze firmly fixed on her filthy hands. Didn't he realize that his slightest touch fired her body? Or didn't he care? Had he ever cared? Or had he simply used her to satisfy his desires? Of course, he hadn't taken anything that she hadn't been more than willing to give, Lucy admitted honestly. He'd made no promises, but then neither had he asked for any. She'd grabbed for a dream and wound up badly burned. Or scraped. Her eyes focused on her badly scratched fingers, and her laugh had a slightly unsteady sound to it.

"Lucy!" Caleb's worried voice cut into her incipient

hysteria. She gulped back the tears that unexpectedly clogged her throat.

"Just reaction," she said, passing off her momentary lapse. "It's kind of you to drive me to my room. I hadn't realized the road went back there."

"It doesn't and I'm not." He swung the big car out onto the main highway.

"Oh?" Lucy frowned at him. "Well, at the risk of sounding overly curious, just where are we going? It may have escaped your notice, but I look like a mess."

"Nothing about you escapes my notice," Caleb replied shortly, then lapsed into silence, leaving Lucy to mull over his words.

"Well, where *are* we going?" she demanded. She was tired, bruised and bloody, to say nothing of the fact that all her happy dreams lay in ruins. She was in no mood to go running around the countryside with him. All she wanted was to crawl into bed—in private. Having to pretend that she didn't know what was going on between him and Beth was taking a heavy toll on her frayed nerves.

"I'm taking you into town to get an X ray of your head," he replied, not put off by her mood.

"What?" Lucy shouted, and winced when her head pounded in protest. "Listen, I know you mean well," she began, trying for a reasonable tone, "but I don't need an X ray. It was a simple, straightforward crack on the head. Certainly nothing to go to a hospital over."

"You're probably right, but nonetheless, we'll get an X ray just to be on the safe side." Caleb's calm tone in no way hid the steel behind his pronouncement.

Lucy bit back an urge to argue. She knew that tone of voice. Caleb had made up his mind, and nothing on earth was going to change it. Under other circumstances she might have enjoyed his concern, high-handed though it was. But the knowledge that he'd finally succumbed to Beth colored the very air she breathed. It was impossible to forget that he merely thought of her as a friend—

in this case, a rather maladroit one who once again needed rescuing from her own stupidity.

To Lucy's relief, the X ray was accomplished in short order. She was assured by the grandfatherly doctor that he'd seen far worse. Lucy roused herself to thank him when he told her that the X rays indicated her head was still in one piece, and that the best thing she could do was go home to bed. Tomorrow she'd be as good as new, he predicted with a cheerful ignorance of the truth.

A nurse helped Lucy dress again and gave her a packet containing two pills along with orders to take them once she'd had a bath.

Lucy found Caleb in conversation with the doctor as she hobbled back into the emergency room's waiting area. Bidding the doctor good-bye, he turned to Lucy. "Come on, woman." He swept her up in his arms. "Let's go."

"Put me down!" she demanded as she noticed the attention they were attracting. "People are staring."

"Let them stare." Caleb chuckled and pulled her closer to his chest. "I'm beginning to get attached to this me-Tarzan, you-Jane routine."

"Oh, for pity's sake!" Lucy groaned and hid her face in his neck in embarrassment.

The sliding doors in the emergency-room entrance opened automatically, and Caleb strode through, depositing her by the side of the car.

"Thank you," Lucy said grudgingly, adding, "I must admit you've got the physique to play Tarzan. You aren't even breathing heavily."

"All that running keeps me in shape." Caleb helped her into the front seat. "Unlike some people I know. But don't worry. Once your bruises heal, we'll get you started on an exercise program."

Lucy pondered his words as he started back to the resort. Could he actually expect to continue with their friendship once he married Beth? She glanced uncertainly at his impassive features. The thought was too horrible to contemplate. To be expected to treat him like a casual acquaintance with the memory of his lovemaking between them? It was impossible. She simply wasn't a good-enough actress.

By the time they'd arrived back at the resort, Lucy was resolved that once they got back to New York City, she was going to make certain she never saw him again. A clean break was always best. She allowed him to help her to her room, all the while trying to think of an excuse to get rid of him without making him suspicious. As it turned out, it wasn't necessary. Beth was waiting in Lucy's room, and Caleb handed her over to Beth with the injunction to help her into bed. Lucy didn't want to see Beth either, but, if it were a choice between Caleb and Beth, she'd take Beth. Beth wasn't nearly as perceptive as Caleb.

"Oh, Lucy, thank you for not telling anyone that I wrecked the jeep. I wouldn't want anyone to know I was such a klutz."

And presumably it didn't matter if Lucy were labeled one. It was hardly Beth's fault that Lucy had been stupid enough to fall in love with Caleb.

"Listen, Beth"—Lucy began to strip off her filthy clothes—"all I want right now is a shower and a nap before dinner. I don't feel up to rehashing the whole fiasco. Just forget it."

"If you say so." Beth paused uncertainly by the door. "But I want you to know that I really appreciate what you've done for me. If you hadn't written that program—"

"Sure, Beth," Lucy hastily interrupted, fearful that Beth was about to tell her about last night's encounter with Caleb. There was no way she could listen to all the details without dissolving into a flood of tears—which would embarrass both of them.

"But, Lucy—"

"Not now!" Lucy snapped, fast losing her control. Why couldn't Beth be a graceful winner and get out?

Because, of course, it hadn't even occurred to Beth that
Lucy had been in the competition. "Beth, I'm sorry."
Lucy forced her voice into level tones. "I ache all over.
I'm not in the mood to talk. So please, just leave me
alone."

"Of course, but I'm glad your head wasn't really hurt."
Beth gave her a stricken look and sidled through the
door.

Lucy flung her shirt into the corner, feeling guilty.
Now Beth was hurt. So let her go to Caleb to get her
tender little feelings soothed, Lucy thought viciously,
then sniffed unhappily at the idea. A tear trickled down
her dirty cheek, to be joined by another and another,
until they became a flood. Lucy didn't even try to stop
them. She went into the shower and let the warm water
wash away the evidence of her misadventure. By the
time she'd dried herself, the tears had dwindled to an
occasional snuffle.

She took the pills the doctor had given her and climbed
into bed. Within minutes she was sound asleep.

It wasn't until early morning that she surfaced from
her drugged sleep. She blinked at the clock in bewil-
derment, unable to believe that it was actually six-thirty
in the morning.

She was relieved to discover that, except for a few
aches and pains, she felt functional. Her head was clear
and her appetite had returned. A quick call to room service brought the promise of coffee and Danish. Lucy
hurried into clothes. While she waited for her order, she
tried to plan. Her accident had had one good result: She
could use it as an excuse to return home. In her present
state of mind, Lucy seriously doubted her ability to keep
up the pretense that she didn't care about Beth and Caleb's engagement.

A sharp knock signaled the arrival of the maid, and
as Lucy opened the door, a sense of déjà vu enveloped
her. It was the friendly maid whose gossip yesterday had

inadvertently brought Lucy's happy world tumbling down about her ears.

"Thank you." Lucy took the tray from the woman, set it on the table, and handed her a tip.

"You're welcome, miss." The woman fidgeted in the doorway, and Lucy eyed her curiously.

"I didn't know you was a friend of that little blonde," she blurted out, "or I never would have told you about what she'd been up to."

"I'm her friend, not her mother," Lucy said. "She does as she pleases."

"Then you won't tell the manager that I was gossiping about the guests?" The woman looked at Lucy hopefully.

"Heavens, no. Besides, after the accident yesterday, I'm not their favorite person."

"Oh, they don't mind anymore. Mr. Bannister fixed that all up. Anyways, that little blonde, she gave me this note to give to you this morning." The woman produced an envelope from her pocket.

"Thank you." Lucy took it, wondering why on earth Beth would be writing to her when she'd see her at breakfast in a few hours.

The maid eyed Lucy, obviously hoping for a further tidbit of gossip, but when none was forthcoming, she left.

Lucy poured herself a cup of hot coffee and sipped it thoughtfully while she looked at Beth's missive. Finally, unable to bear the suspense, she slit it open. One glance was enough to convince her she'd made a mistake. Beth's note was short and to the point. It said she was going to Nevada to get married, since there was no waiting period there. Beth softened the blow by profusely thanking Lucy for making it all possible.

"My God!" Lucy's voice trembled as she scanned the note again, hoping to see something she'd originally missed—but it was crystal-clear. Caleb was so besotted that he'd whisked Beth off to Nevada to get married.

"Damn!" Lucy crumbled the paper and threw it across the room. They must have left right after she went to bed last night. They could even be married by now. Lucy tried in vain to remember where Nevada was in relation to Wyoming, but couldn't.

Lucy glared at the cream-colored walls, suddenly overwhelmed by the need to escape this room where she and Caleb had spent such an exquisite afternoon. With no destination in mind, Lucy hurried outside, totally oblivious to both the chill morning air and her lingering aches.

She needed to think, but her thoughts gave her no peace. Visions of Beth's slim white body locked against Caleb's bronzed muscles made her feel faintly sick. Round and round her thoughts tore, a poisonous blend of envy, jealousy, and raging unhappiness.

You should have had enough sense to have stayed married to Marcus, she castigated herself. He might not have been able to raise her to the heights, but by the same token, he never made her feel as if her world had come to a splintering halt.

Lucy viciously kicked at a pebble, wishing it were the idiot who'd proclaimed that it was better to have loved and lost than to have never loved at all. At least before, she'd been content. Now all contentment had disappeared into a seething caldron of desperation.

At last, Lucy's aching muscles managed to penetrate even the depths of her unhappiness, and she reluctantly turned back.

She let herself into her room and sagged wearily against the back of the closed door, only to jump in fright at the sound of an angry voice.

"Where the hell have you been!" Caleb demanded. "The maid said you left hours ago."

"Hours?" Lucy murmured, wondering whether she was sufficiently in control of herself to risk offering him congratulations. She hadn't realized Nevada was so close.

Unless, of course, they'd flown. Lucy remembered his penchant for small aircraft.

"It's nine o'clock!" he shouted. "You were supposed to stay in bed. Haven't you any sense? You're white as a sheet—at least, the parts that aren't black and blue are!"

Caleb's harsh words began to penetrate Lucy's numbed senses, and she felt the beginnings of temper. How dare he sneak off to marry her best friend and then come back to yell at her?

"Shut up!" Lucy snapped.

"What?" Caleb's brilliant blue eyes deepened in shock at her belligerent tone.

"I said shut up," Lucy obligingly repeated. "What I do is none of your concern."

"Like hell it isn't!" Caleb started toward her, and Lucy quailed before his six and a half feet of livid, masculine outrage.

"You listen to me, Caleb Bannister!" Lucy gritted out. "You gave up all rights to tell me what to do when you married Beth."

"When I *what*?" he bellowed.

"She told me." Lucy sank down on the bed and gulped, praying she wouldn't burst into tears and reveal how much she cared.

"She told you we were eloping?" he asked, suddenly calm.

"Was it supposed to be a secret?" Lucy quipped. "I hate to be the one to break it to you, but Beth can't keep a secret to save her soul. She sent me a letter." She retrieved the crumpled sheet from across the room.

Caleb smoothed it out, reading the hasty scrawl.

"Good Lord!" He whistled. "So that explains it."

"Explains what?"

"The letter this morning from Joel saying that he'd decided against drilling the wells himself. He said he was going to sell the mineral rights to one of the big oil companies instead."

"But he was determined to drill himself." Lucy frowned.

"Not at the cost of something he wanted even more." Caleb sank down on the bed beside her and Lucy scooted away in self-disgust. Even knowing he was married, she couldn't help responding to him.

"I think I missed something somewhere. This is all very interesting, but none of it seems to tie together."

"The key is Beth's visit to me night before last," he said. "Or, more accurately, her visit was the catalyst."

"But why did your marrying Beth make Joel decide not to drill?"

"You remind me of a desk plaque my sister once gave me. It said, 'My mind's made up; don't confuse me with the facts.'" He chuckled.

"It isn't funny!" Lucy snapped, furious that he could be amused at the situation.

"It's hilarious, love, and, furthermore, I am not married to your flighty little friend."

Lucy's eyes widened as she savored the feeling of sheer joy that flooded her body. He hadn't married Beth! But . . .

She frowned as she remembered the letter. It had been quite specific.

"Then who did she marry?"

"Joel," Caleb replied patiently. "He took one look at her that first night and fell like a ton of bricks. He's been begging her to marry him ever since. Why do you suppose he invited her out here, if not to get time alone with her?"

"Then the plane trip was a setup," Lucy accused him. "You purposely arranged it so they could fly out together."

"Joel arranged it. And why shouldn't I have agreed? I'd much rather spend time with you than him."

Not much of a compliment, as compliments went, Lucy decided and then dismissed it in her desire to unravel the story of Beth's elopement.

"If Beth was all set to marry Joel, why did she spend the night with you?" Lucy scowled to keep her lip from trembling.

"She didn't spend the night with me. She got the maid to let her in, then waited for me. I didn't go back to my room until after one. We spent about twenty minutes talking, then she left."

"Oh?" Lucy was dying to ask what had been said, but she didn't have the right to ask. She wasn't sure just how far Caleb's patience at her prying would extend.

He picked up her hand and, turning it over, began to lightly trace designs on her palm.

Lucy shifted restlessly and tried to pull her hand away. She wanted some answers first, and she knew that if he continued touching her, she'd soon forget everything but the pleasure he was evoking.

"And you seemed like such a sensible soul," Caleb chided her. "How did you ever let yourself get involved with anything so scatterbrained as Beth's plan to marry me?"

"You figured it out?" She winced. She'd hoped she could keep that particular piece of information to herself.

"No, I didn't." He gave up his designs on her hand and began to nuzzle her neck, carefully avoiding a long, red scratch under her ear. "I was so busy thinking up ways and means of seducing you that I totally missed Beth's plans."

"But then how . . ."

"That's why Beth came to my room. Joel was pushing her for an answer. As long as there was any chance of marrying my money, she didn't want to accept him. So she draped herself on my bed and tried to seduce me. When I told her in no uncertain terms that I wasn't interested, she lost her composure, and the whole story came tumbling out."

Lucy shot him a wary glance. "And you weren't interested in her? But the computer indicated it was a sure thing."

"And you're a sucker for a pitch from a friend." Caleb snorted. "Lady, you need a keeper."

"It wasn't all that bad an idea," Lucy insisted. "And the computer application was fascinating . . . But why didn't you fall for Beth?" Lucy asked curiously. "She should have been made to order for you."

"Because by then I'd met you." He gently pushed her down on the bed and began to unfasten her shirt buttons. "I took one look at you chugging around the park like a runaway steam engine and I was lost."

"You didn't *do* anything," Lucy said doubtfully, remembering how he hadn't even looked at her.

"I was desperately trying to figure out how to approach you. I hadn't seen you there before, so I knew you didn't live around the park—and from the way you were huffing and puffing, I also knew that you'd never make it around again. When that ill-tempered little Pekingese tripped you up, I could have bought him a steak. It gave me a chance to introduce myself."

"But I'm not your type," she insisted.

"Lucy . . ." Caleb finished unfastening her buttons and pushed her shirt open. "Your program concluded that I dated those women because they were small and blonde, but I dated them because they were sophisticated women who no more wanted commitment than I did. But even if I'd been attracted to Beth, it wouldn't have gone beyond a date."

"Why?" Lucy shivered as his hands unfastened her bra. He began to lightly rub the tip of one breast between his thumb and forefinger. "Don't," she protested. "I'm trying to think."

"I wouldn't, if I were you. You're dangerous when you think. As for your question: because I'm much too old to be satisfied with spending my time gazing soulfully into a pair of green eyes, no matter how beautiful they are. It takes a little conversation, too, and Beth froze up like a clam every time I came near."

"True." She gasped as his fingers slid under the waistband of her jeans. "She'll do much better with Joel. She's not afraid of him."

"He's the one who should be afraid!" Caleb said tartly. "She made him give up his plans to drill before she would marry him. She'll lead him around by the nose."

"If he's happy—" Lucy broke off as her stomach gave a loud rumble.

"Good Lord, woman." Caleb sat back in astonishment. "When was the last time you fed that poor thing?"

Lucy frowned, trying to remember. "Day before yesterday, I think. It seemed that every time I went to eat, someone dropped ghastly news on me. But I'm definitely going to breakfast now."

"Oh, dear." He looked penitent. "I hesitate to spring this on you . . ."

"Yes?" Lucy eyed him warily.

"We're flying out of here in exactly twenty minutes, so you'd better get up."

"We're going home?" Lucy fought down a sense of disappointment. Now that she'd finally gotten rid of Beth and her mad schemes, she'd hoped to enjoy the remainder of the weekend with Caleb.

"No, to Nevada." He grabbed her hand, pulled her to her feet, and began buttoning her shirt.

"Are we going to their wedding?" she asked. She still didn't know exactly where Nevada was, nor did she care. She'd have happily trailed along behind Caleb if he'd decided to explore the Arctic Circle.

"No. Our own." He urged her toward the door.

"Our *what*?" Lucy stopped dead and stared at him in amazement. "But you haven't asked me!"

"And I'm not going to." He gave her a crooked smile. "You might say no, and I love you too much to take your rejection with a stiff upper lip. I'd probably do something criminal like kidnap you and not let you go until you agreed to marry me."

Lucy smiled euphorically. She didn't understand how this miracle had happened, but she wasn't questioning it. Caleb loved her. It was there in the anxious expression deep in his brilliant blue eyes. She simply accepted it as a gift from the gods.

"You wouldn't have had to do anything that drastic," she said softly. "Haven't you figured out yet that all you have to do is to kiss me and I'll agree to anything? I love you, Caleb Bannister." Lucy's words were a vow. "You're everything I ever wanted in a man. You're kind, intelligent, gentle, humorous, a fantastic lover, and best of all"—her eyes gleamed impishly—"you're taller than I am."

"Oh, Lucy." His choked voice told her the depths of his feelings as he wrapped her in a suffocating embrace.

"Miss, you—" The door opened and the gossipy maid blundered in. "Gracious me!" she gasped. "Don't tell me he's cuddling up to you, too!"

"Yes," Lucy said, laughing, "but I'm the last cuddlee he gets. I'm going to marry him and reform his wandering ways."

"Really!" Her nose twitched with excitement. "Congratulations, I'm sure!" the maid called over her shoulder as she hurried out.

"I wonder what she wanted," Lucy mused.

"I don't know, and I don't care. It's your obvious duty to make an honest man out of me. Since our plane leaves in fifteen minutes, we've just time to pick up a picnic breakfast."

Lucy put her hand trustingly in Caleb's and sighed with happiness. Her faith in the computer had been badly shaken—but somehow she was relieved to discover that matches were still made in heaven.

WATCH FOR 6 NEW TITLES EVERY MONTH!

Second Chance at Love

All of the above titles are $1.75 per copy except where noted

SK-41a

WHAT READERS SAY ABOUT
SECOND CHANCE AT LOVE BOOKS

"I can't begin to thank you for the many, many hours of pure bliss I have received from the wonderful SECOND CHANCE [AT LOVE] books. Everyone I talk to lately has admitted their preference for SECOND CHANCE [AT LOVE] over all the other lines."
—*S. S., Phoenix, AZ**

"Hurrah for Berkley . . . the butterfly and its wonderful SECOND CHANCE AT LOVE."
—*G. B., Mount Prospect, IL**

"Thank you, thank you, thank you—I just had to write to let you know how much I love SECOND CHANCE AT LOVE . . ."
—*R. T., Abbeville, LA**

"It's so hard to wait 'til it's time for the next shipment . . . I hope your firm soon considers adding to the line."
—*P. D., Easton, PA**

"SECOND CHANCE AT LOVE is fantastic. I have been reading romances for as long as I can remember—and I enjoy SECOND CHANCE [AT LOVE] the best."
—*G. M., Quincy, IL**

*Names and addresses available upon request